CANDY
in the
DUMPSTER

edited by bill breedlove

MARTIN MUNDT

JOHN EVERSON

BILL BREEDLOVE

JAY BONANSINGA

DARKARTS
B O O K S

For more information on this and other Dark Arts Books titles, visit www.darkartsbooks.com or e-mail sales@darkartsbooks.com.

All stories are printed or reprinted here with permission of the authors.

Cover photos, collage and book design copyright © 2006 by John Everson, except front cover photo of Jade Paris by MinkyBlink and back cover and inside photos of the authors by Joe Heinen.

"Introduction: Candy in the Dumpster" copyright © 2006 by Mort Castle.

"A Perfect Plan" copyright © 2004 by Martin Mundt.
Originally published in *Masque of the Small Town Oddball*. (Iguana Publications, Fall 2004).

"The Cure" copyright © 2006 by Martin Mundt.

"Babies Is Smart" copyright © 2006 by Martin Mundt.

"The White House" copyright © 2006 by John Everson.

"Swallowing the Pill" copyright © 2000 by John Everson.
Originally published in *Cage of Bones & Other Deadly Obsessions*. (Delirium Books, Oct. 2000)

"Pumpkin Head" copyright © 1999 by John Everson.
Originally published in *Grue Magazine* #19 (Hell's Kitchen Productions, 1999).

"The Lost Collection" copyright © 2003 by Bill Breedlove.
Originally published in *Most Curious* (MTD Press, 2003).

"Drowning in the Sea of Love" copyright © 2006 by Bill Breedlove.

"Free to Good Home" copyright © 2006 by Bill Breedlove.

"Animal Rites" copyright © 1995 by Jay Bonansinga.
Originally published in *Cemetery Dance* #22 (CD Publications, Winter 1995).

"Stash" copyright © 2003 by Jay Bonansinga.
Originally appeared in *Cemetery Dance* #44 (CD Publications, 2003).

"Deal Memo" copyright © 2006 by Jay Bonansinga.

Printed in the United States of America.
First Edition, May 2006
Third Edition, July 2008
ISBN-13: 978-0-9779686-0-2
ISBN-10: 0-9779686-0-X
10 9 8 7 6 5 4 3

DARKARTS

B O O K S

ACKNOWLEDGEMENTS

We did it our way.

CONTENTS

Introduction:

CANDY IN THE DUMPSTER

Once upon a time, having been asked to write an introduction to this book of fine horror stories by four fine authors, I'd have said, "Really good book here. Read it."

But in my maturity (dotage?) I have become something of the academic, and that straightforward, "here-you-go, how's-by-you?" approach is no longer what is expected of me, so...

In an era of post-neo-modern deconstructionist pseudo-empirical non-epistolary Horror Literature, it is generally agreed that a good story collection should be not just individual works of fiction stuck between two covers. Rather, there should be a *unifying* aspect, (see Colonius of Powell, *The Lower Tracts*, translated by Roman Gnose), whether of theme, tone, mood, sub-text, or mindless use of the Cyrillic alphabet.

Candy in the Dumpster is a better-than-good story collection. And as one might expect, such a work therefore has more than one "unifying aspect" (See "*Unitas Johnikus* and the Milieu of Parson Monet"). As we cannot call a mere coincidence George W. Bush's having the same last name as a previous President, although the latter had a measurable IQ, we would be unwise to dismiss the fact that Monsieurs (Pronounced *Mess-youse*) Everson, Mundt, Bonansinga, and Breedlove have all at one time or another in their lives resided in a dumpster. Though the "New Critics," circa 1948, sought to separate the writing from the writer, we now recognize that just as Hemingway did too shoot lions, so, too, did Breedlove have soy sauce splashed on his chest in the days when he resided in the alley domicile behind the *Panda Express*. Furthermore, the name *Mundt*, when rendered in the Cyrillic alphabet, means "dumpster"; as the monk Methodius, friend and companion to Cyril, explains in the seminal text, *No Such Thing as A Bad Boy*:

> Mundt means 'dumpster' for there were dumpsters aplenty in those days.
> Yea.
>
> Verily.

Then there is the Chicago connection. Chicago is the "city of the big shoulders," says Carl Sandburg, and it is the "city on the make" says Nelson Algren, but it is for literary scholars other than I to explain how it is Martin (Mundt), Jay (Bonansinga), Bill (Breedlove), and John (Everson) never met Carl Sandburg nor Nelson Algren, although to his sort of credit, Bonansinga does claim to have watched the film *The Man with the Golden Arm* after a losing round of "Truth or Dare."

To understand the essential commonality that unites these stories and their writers, I turn to my wife, who, upon hearing John Everson read a short story at the Midwest Literary Festival (See "My Kinda Town, Aurora Is," *Journal of Midwestern Depravity and Fellowship*, August 2006), remarked, "He's really funny."

They all are, Mundt, Bonansinga, Everson, and Breedlove.

And though each is a unique perspective and unique voice, they all have that "tongue in cheek" (not necessarily one's own), satirical, never say "die" when you can say "maim" kind of thinking that we find in those works of horror likely to reside and resound within the reader's consciousness for a long, long time.

I think the punny Crypt Keeper introducing his ghoulish EC Tales would appreciate the humor of these fine Chicagoans.

I think Charles Beaumont, who penned the classic line "No

Fowl had ever looked more posthumous" and Roald *Switch, Bitch* Dahl, and especially Mr. Sardonic Himself Robert Bloch, who had the heart of a small boy which he kept in a jar on his desk, would recognize and applaud the insightful humor and horror of these four fine writers – because humor and horror not only go together, they are damned near synonyms.

So, then, have some fears and have some funnies, and have a fine old time with *Candy in the Dumpster*.

–Mort Castle
UnderEndowed Folding Chair of
Literature, Ludwig Von Drake U
and Semi-Finalist, Publishers
Clearing House Sweepstakes

Martin Mundt *has published a collection of short stories called* The Crawling Abattoir *through Twilighttales.com. His second collection,* The Dark Underbelly of Hymns, *was published by Deliriumbooks.com in March 2006.*

He has published recent stories in Bone Ballet, Spooks!, *and* Masque of the Small Town Oddball. *His play,* The Jackie Sexknife Show, *was produced in Chicago in 2003.*

His website is www.MartinMundt.com.

A PERFECT PLAN

As she slid off his knife, she dragged all his anger away with her, and then he felt – nothing.

Well, not exactly nothing. He felt screwed.

Viki's blood ran down the blade and dripped off the point onto her body, which was now lying on the kitchen floor at his feet. No, not really the point of the blade, Bobby noticed. The point of the blade had broken off, somewhere inside Viki, probably on a rib.

He hadn't meant to kill her, not that she hadn't had it coming. He'd had a real bad day at the warehouse and on deliveries, an even worse day with his co-workers and his customers, and worst of all, he'd almost punched out his boss, except he'd backed down, like always, and that made him feel like – made him feel like his shriveled balls were nailed up on his boss' trophy wall, right next to his perfect 300 game bowling plaque.

So today wasn't a good day for Viki to spring on him that she was pregnant. They had agreed they wouldn't have kids. Bobby had been totally upfront about kids. Sure, he'd marry her if she wanted, in a year or two, when he got his feet on the ground; but no kids, and then she goes and stops taking the pill without telling him, and boom, there's a kid on the way – his kid – and she starts right in leaning on him about getting married right away, like this weekend. She shouldn't have pushed him, but she shined at pushing, and most of the time she acted like she had his balls nailed to the wall over their headboard – on her side of the bed, of course.

"So, either shit or get off the pot, Bobby," she'd yelled, hands on hips, glaring at him. "What's it gonna be?"

Bobby dropped the knife, which bounced off her bare belly and clattered to the floor. She kept staring at the ceiling.

He felt panic start to slice up his gut. Yeah, now he was really screwed. He bent down and grabbed Viki's ankles and dragged her to the back door, then stopped. A trail of blood streaked across the kitchen floor. The knife still lay next to the pool of blood at the end of the trail. He went back and got the knife, then slipped the blade into the low waistband of Viki's jeans. He grabbed the doorknob, then stopped again.

Shit. He should dig a grave first, before he started dragging her body around the yard. He took his hand off the doorknob, leaving a slop of blood behind. Shit. He had to remember to clean everything he touched. But first, he needed a shovel. Or maybe he should cut up the body first. In which case he needed a saw. But then blood would get on everything, so he needed to cut the body up in the bathtub upstairs.

No, wait. What he really needed was a 55-gallon drum of acid. No, wait, shit. Where was he gonna get acid? He needed to get his propane torch out of the garage and burn off her fingerprints and her face and her tattoos and then cut up her body and then bury the pieces separately in the woods south of town and then clean the blood out of the bathtub and the bathroom and the stairs and the kitchen, and then bury the knife.

No, wait, maybe he should keep the knife, since it was part of a set, and if one went missing then it would call attention to itself, except that the point had broken off inside her, and shit, he didn't know what to do with the knife, except for sure he'd have to say that she'd gone out somewhere – he didn't know where – and just never came back. Just disappeared. Women disappeared all the time. She must've been kidnapped, maybe murdered, by – Satanists, so they could use the baby for human sacrifice rituals and – no, wait. Shit. He probably shouldn't mention the baby at all. Keep it simple, stupid. Yeah, K.I.S.S. He giggled at the thought of kissing Viki now.

What's the best way to clean off blood? He knew the cops had ways to find blood traces. He watched CSI. He stared at his hands clutching Viki's ankles – blood smearing her skin. His fingerprints on her skin. Shit. What else didn't he know? He stared at the bloody boot-prints on the floor.

Shit. OK, so, dump her in the woods, call her in missing, and clean up. No, wait. Clean up first, then call her in missing; but, call it in right away, or wait a day or two? How long did it take to cut up a body? And should he say that everything had been going great between them, or should he give her a motive for leaving, say she'd been kinda restless lately?

No. Shit, no.

He closed his eyes, forced his thoughts to stop swirling.

No. No cutting, no burying, no Satanists. That kind of shit never worked anyway. Hell, he was her boyfriend. He lived with her. He would be the first one the cops looked at, maybe the only one. And they'd find the body, sure as shit; they'd find evidence; they'd find holes in his story. They'd figure it all out pretty quick. He watched COURT TV and COPS.

Shit. Now he was really, truly, one-hundred-percent, grade-A screwed with a capital S. Why the fuck hadn't he just knocked her around a little instead of killing her?

So. What to do? He needed a plan. A good plan. No loose ends. Hell, he needed a great plan.

He stared at her belly, at the knife stuck in her waistband, the handle making an X with her hipbone, and he wished she wasn't dead, really wished he hadn't killed her, when –

– when, just like that, the plan came to him. Simple and doable and perfect.

He dropped Viki's legs with a thump-thump and went upstairs to get his pistol.

*   *   *   *   *

Bobby peeked around the corner of the 7-11 into the alley, then pulled his head back. Darryl sat in his police car, like always, probably eating cheese fries. Bobby looked at his watch. 11:14 p.m. Didn't matter really. The town of Newton rolled up the sidewalks at about ten. Bobby felt the bricks prickle his back through his shirt as he leaned against the wall.

He didn't look forward to this, but he couldn't think of any other way to fix everything. He took a deep breath and slipped around the corner. The 7-11's Dumpster smelled like a sonuvabitch, the stink like a force field, and Bobby walked wide around it, making for the driver's side of the police car.

Darryl had his window rolled down. Bobby smelled cheese fries. He grinned. Good old predictable Darryl. Bobby lifted his pistol until the muzzle touched Darryl right behind his left ear. Darryl twitched and started to turn and speak.

Bobby pulled the trigger before he could see Darryl's eyes. The shot sounded like a cough. Trace evidence splotted all over the inside of the car like a bouquet of bloody flowers. Darryl slumped over, sprawled across his computer console.

Bobby opened the driver's door. The idiot-alarm went off – BONG-BONG-BONG – because Darryl still had his keys in the ignition. Bobby jumped at the sound and banged his head on the door-frame. The pistol went off, shooting Darryl through the leg. The shot flashed like lightning and sounded much louder confined inside the car.

"Shit," said Bobby. He jerked the keys out of the ignition, and the bonging stopped. He took Darryl's revolver and shotgun, then closed the door.

He stood next to the car and listened for a minute, clutching Darryl's shotgun and pistol against his chest with his left arm.

He heard nothing.

OK. That hadn't been so bad.

He started walking the two blocks to Sheriff Gault's house. He figured no one would stop him. By eleven, everyone in Newton had usually already fallen asleep, and even if anyone did see him walking around with two pistols and a shotgun, he knew he was doing something that no one – absolutely no one – in Newton could possibly figure out. His plan was that good.

People left their doors unlocked in Newton, so when he got to the Sheriff's house, he just walked right in. He didn't turn on the lights. He let his eyes get used to the quiet darkness before he crept up the stairs to the bedrooms.

The Sheriff and his wife Marge didn't wake up while he stood over their bed. He knew they had a kid, down the hall in another bedroom, maybe eleven or twelve. Gary, he thought the kid's name was. So he didn't want to make any unnecessary noise.

He slipped a cushion out from under the Sheriff's pants on a chair next to the bed. He pressed it over Sheriff Gault's face, pushed the muzzle into it and fired through the padding.

Surprisingly, the idea worked pretty well. A little flash, a little thoomf, and he pulled the cushion away, and Sheriff Gault's head looked like – well, Bobby didn't see any point in dwelling on what Sheriff Gault's head looked like any more.

Next, he did Marge Gault. Flash, thoomf. He left the cushion covering her face.

He didn't need a cushion for Gary, because there was no one left to hear anything.

He closed the front door behind him. He'd just eliminated Newton's entire law enforcement community, and armed himself with another shotgun and pistol to boot. So, with no investigators, there could be no Viki Ann Rollins murder investigation.

Except –

There was always Ethel Clack. She was Sheriff Gault's secretary, the department's dispatcher. She was a cop, almost. At least she knew how to dial the State Police. And Doctor Davis too. He did coroner's stuff, wrote out death certificates. He had written out Bobby's mother's certificate two years back. He knew cop stuff too.

But neither of them lived far away. No one lived far away from anyone else in Newton.

Bobby started walking.

*   *   *   *   *

Killing Viki's mother was a no-brainer. Mrs. Rollins had never liked Bobby anyway. She always told Viki that she could do better – and this was when Bobby was standing right there in the room with them.

He let Mrs. Rollins wake up before he did her, with the shotgun, and with more shells than were strictly necessary, but there was, after all, a certain measure of personal feeling involved with Mrs. Rollins.

Twelve-twenty-two clicked over on Mrs. Rollins' bedside clock as Bobby's hands stopped vibrating from the shotgun blasts. He took stock of his evening.

Viki. Darryl. Sheriff Gault. Marge. Gary. Ethel. Doctor Davis. Harold Standish, the editor and publisher of the Newton Pantograph-Leader. Jim Kastner, a part-timer at the Pantograph-

Leader who fancied himself an investigative reporter. Fred Alton, the radio guy. He'd popped Davey Spender in the 7-11 because he'd wanted something to drink, and Davey saw the blood and the guns, and, well, why the hell not by that point? They always overcharged at the 7-11 anyway. He'd done Heather, Doctor Davis' nurse, because she was bound to notice that Doctor Davis was dead. Then he did the three volunteer firemen – Bill, Johnny and the other guy – so they wouldn't do any clever emergency stuff, and OK, that added up to what? Fifteen?

No, sixteen. He'd done Karl the postman too, because he figured Karl was a Fed, and Federal involvement was a complication he didn't need.

But he didn't need to kill everyone in town. That would just be crazy. There just had to be no one left alive who could finger him, who could say that he and Viki didn't always get along great, who could even identify him, and then he could fall between the cracks. So he really only needed to kill anyone who knew him.

Which, when he thought about it, was pretty much everyone in town.

Shit.

OK. New plan. Kill everyone.

He fired up Doctor Davis' Lincoln Town Car. He'd gotten tired of walking, and besides, he had a couple of dozen guns by now, too many to carry. The Doc also had a Newton phone book in the car, which was a stroke of luck. Bobby opened it on the passenger seat.

Abrams, Donald.

Bobby smiled. Donnie Abrams was his boss.

* * * * *

Small towns didn't come much smaller than Newton, until you started working your way through it person by person. The WELCOME TO NEWTON sign at the town-line read: Population 283, and that was probably accurate, give or take. Bobby crossed off names in the phone book until he got to Thomas Yarnell. No Z's in Newton. He'd never noticed that before.

He could bury Viki's murder in a whole bunch of other murders, so that no one would be able to put it all together, because none of it would make any fucking sense at all, like half-a-dozen slasher movies all spliced together.

He smiled. Christ, what a great plan.

Except –

– he remembered that guy on CSI who could use goddamn bugs to figure out times of death, and that would lead to timelines, and timelines would be like arrows pointing right at Viki – and him.

Shit.

OK. New plan. Get rid of all the evidence. Yeah. He reached forward to start up the Lincoln, then stopped.

Except that the amount of evidence had sort of mushroomed on him in the past few hours, and his inability to get rid of the evidence for Viki's murder alone had been the reason for his plan in the first place.

Shit. He leaned back in the driver's seat. He couldn't bury 283 dead bodies in the woods south of town. Or could he? No, no, he couldn't, and in a million years he couldn't clean up all the blood either – he hadn't exactly been stingy with the shotgun, and then, when he'd found that chainsaw at Earl Twohy's place, well, he just hadn't been able to resist super-sizing the carnage, because he knew his plan, and chaos was his friend.

So what could he do?

He thought about it, and, just like that –

OK. New plan.

He grinned. He fired up the Lincoln.

*　*　*　*　*

The highway looked empty from the gas station. The Sun brightened the sky behind the low hills east of town.

OK. The plan had been set in motion. Time for him to make himself scarce. He pulled the Lincoln away from the pumps.

He hadn't particularly wanted to kill the kid working at the gas station, but the plan didn't allow for any deviation.

He hit the on-ramp just as the Sun topped the hills, and the sudden glare blinded him. He never saw the SUV speeding down the hill until the last second. A horn blared. The SUV swerved into the other lane and kept going, doing ninety at least.

"Shit," said Bobby, horsing the Lincoln onto the shoulder and screeching to a stop.

Just then the firebombs – all made from the gasoline he'd taken from the gas station after he'd killed the kid – started to go off in Newton, booming explosions Bobby felt rock the Lincoln.

The driver of the SUV must have seen the explosions. His brake lights flashed once, but he didn't stop.

OK. So maybe using firebombs to burn up all the evidence wasn't such a great idea. Thirty or forty explosions had rippled through the ground by now. The SUV driver could hardly have missed it, and he could probably identify Bobby's car too, coming out of town just as all hell broke loose. The Doc's Lincoln was lime-green, after all, with vanity plates that read LOOK AT ME.

Shit.

OK. New plan. Bobby had sixty-two guns, maybe a thousand rounds of ammunition, a couple of spare firebombs, some acid he'd picked up for the hell of it, and a chainsaw in the trunk. He floored the Lincoln and took off after the SUV.

Newton fireballed into the sky in his rearview mirror.

THE CURE

The cockroaches fled the room.

Tommy figured that was a bad sign.

He listened to them scurry, like sand blowing across the floor. They flowed over his exposed face as he lay in bed, the blanket fluttering on top of him under their wavering weight.

He needed a hit, but he forced himself not to move.

The stench charged after them, clogging his nose like the smell of ten wet, sick lions all jammed together in a single cage. He started to gag, but strangled the puke back down. No sound. No movement. He gave no sign he existed. He allowed one eye to open a slit.

The Cure crouched in a dark corner of Tommy's studio apartment. Its two eyes shone like polished night-sky in the midnight shadows, huge as hubcaps, round and flat like something hauled up out of an ocean trench. It didn't blink.

Tommy hadn't heard it come in; even as fucked-up sick as he was, he figured he should've noticed that.

A single streak of neon from the liquor-store sign outside his window hummed through the curtains, running like a vein across the floor in a place that was mostly played out of light. White neon slipped into green, slid into red, faded to white – each color in turn staining the Cure's talons, the longest eighteen inches of samurai-sword curve, the middle one a butcher knife, the smallest six inches of honed switchblade – a real reaper of a claw-hand. Blood, or puke, or feces – or maybe all three – matted its black, shaggy fur.

It scraped a bright, deep scar in the hardwood floor with the ice-pick tip of its samurai talon – dragging the tip back and forth, back and forth – grinding the wood as regular as a countdown.

Tommy had pawned his clock radio ages ago, and his watch too. But now he listened as the talon carved the passage of time back into his brain.

Tommy couldn't see its other arm in the shadows. Maybe it didn't have one.

The Cure killed. That was all. Just killed. Maybe it didn't need two arms to do that.

The street had hung the nickname on the beast. Name the boogeyman and have power over it, except of course no one on the street had any power over the Cure. Tommy figured if it had any kind of real name, probably only a few government types knew what it was. He figured the Cure was an anti-drug program – just a very top-secret, hush-hush, black budget, plausibly deniable kind of program.

Drugs called out to the Cure. The beast didn't want the drugs themselves, and it didn't really want Tommy either; what it wanted was Tommy's blood sweetened by the drugs.

As long as Tommy stayed clean, he was OK, he was safe. Which was why the beast was called the Cure, of course. The fear of it kept you clean; or else it came in the night – like here, like now – and ripped you to pieces to drink your blood.

Either way you got cured.

Tommy moved; the Cure moved. Except Tommy was just stretching underneath the blanket. His muscles burned and tingled as if they were crawling all over his skeleton, looking for someplace comfortable to lie down and die. He'd sweated himself dry hours ago. He felt like his body wasn't complete – and only ezy could make him passably human again. Ezy was Tommy's drug of choice.

It was called tri-di-something-methyl-something or otheride. Tommy had never been able to negotiate his way through one continuous pronunciation of it. He was a junkie, not a chemist. First it had been called eye-chart on the street; then e-c for short; then ezy. Only it wasn't easy.

He had tried cold turkey for the past six months, but it hadn't worked – a half-year of his mind slipping inside reality, sliding outside again. Tommy couldn't remember most of it now. Six months of the pain of being born into a new life, and the end result was stillbirth. He still craved ezy.

The Cure stopped scraping. Its muscles tightened, as if it could feel Tommy thinking about the drug, as if it were preparing to launch itself on him.

Tommy felt the room shiver from the Cure's muscles coiling – the floor, the walls, even the air between them humming with anticipation, as if the two of them were connected.

It knew he was empty and weak; it knew that the first thing ezy had eaten away inside him had been his spine.

But what it didn't know was that these drugs were cut with some special stuff meant to keep him safe from the Cure. Yessir, special anti-cure stuff. So he had nothing to be afraid of. He could take these drugs, and the Cure would leave him be, pass him over, vanish into thin, untroubled air.

That is, assuming he had gotten the truth from Gaspar along with the vial.

*   *   *   *   *

"Tommy, my friend, you look like a dead man!" Gaspar had said, smiling from just inside the shadows of the alley off 54th Street. His teeth were perfect enameled white, except for one gold front tooth.

"Hi, Gaspar." Tommy nodded, sidling up to the alley's edge. He shoved his hands into his pockets, his tensed fists like huge, cramped, denim muscles on his thighs.

Tommy stared at the gold tooth. He'd seen Gaspar slide it off once, like a gold sheath. Gaspar slipped back and forth between the street and the mainstream, one to earn his money, and the other to spend it. Gold tooth for the street; white for the mainstream. Well, at least Tommy thought he'd seen Gaspar slide the tooth off once. He wasn't sure about a lot of things any more.

"Sure," said Tommy. "I guess." He hadn't really been paying attention.

Gaspar shook his head. "Tommy, Tommy, Tommy, my backsliding friend. You just can't stay away from Gaspar, can you? I am touched. Truly touched. How long has it been anyway? My wallet says too long, but it's a fine day when I can see an old friend from the old neighborhood. There's not a lot of old in this business, Tommy." He grinned. "So what can I do for you?"

Tommy tore his stare away from the tooth. Gaspar wore a black jogging suit with red racing stripes, but the colors were faded. Tommy could almost have sworn that they were the same clothes he'd seen Gaspar in six months ago. He'd moved his sales territory too, a dozen or so blocks east, into a nicer neighborhood, migrating ahead of the Cure in search of live junkies. Tommy had had a time finding him.

The street here was empty, though, just like the old neighborhood. Junkies died, of course; it was what junkies did, only never before in such numbers. Tommy had heard that the Cure, having nearly exhausted the vein of hard users, had taken to prescription drug users instead, preying on drugstores like methadone – a brute being incapable of making the fine distinctions between socially acceptable – even socially necessary – drugs, and socially unacceptable ones. Tommy couldn't decide if that was more likely to be a baseless rumor or an urban legend, but the drugstore on the corner was boarded up.

"Is it safe?" said Tommy. He looked around. "I mean, are there – you know – around?" Tommy had no doubt there were eyes watching them – beasts watching Gaspar the way lions watched watering holes.

"Of course there are," said Gaspar. "Too many beasts, and not enough junkies." He nodded at the corner drugstore. "But enough Xanax and Prozac and Viagra for a smorgasbord." He leaned in close to Tommy and whispered. "The cops said it was a robbery gone bad." He laughed – a weird high-pitched giggle like a blond, blue-eyed, little-girl Satanist. "Absolutely, officer," singsonged Gaspar, "a robbery with twelve solid citizens ripped limb from limb, a robbery with guzzled blood, a robbery with no money gone." He winked at Tommy. "Too many beasts and not enough junkies, Tommy. So you can see why I'm so immeasurably happy to see you."

"You saw it?" said Tommy.

"I didn't see a thing," said Gaspar. He tapped his nose with one finger. "But I can smell." He sniffed. "Blood and death for days afterwards. But tell me, where've you been these past six bloody months?"

"Uh," said Tommy, "around." He glanced up and down the street – the bright, open, sunlit, unshadowed noonday street. He scrunched his head down between his shoulders. He shivered. He shivered all the time now. He couldn't even remember what it was like to be warm.

In truth, Tommy couldn't really remember where he'd been. Withdrawal had laid him out, shredded reality with hallucinations, blackouts and visions. He thought he remembered being abducted by aliens two or three times. Shadowy alien doctors with big heads and goggles strapped him to a table beneath blinding lights and probed him, inserting things into his body, removing other things. He was almost sure he remembered his kidneys being stolen, waking up day after day in a bathtub filled with ice cubes, his abdomen a cuneiform of freshly stitched incisions. He knew he had only two kidneys, but the scalpel-wielding shadows had entered him two, three, a dozen times. He'd drifted in and out of reality – or maybe never really in. He hadn't known what was what for months, and now – now he just knew emptiness.

"Just around," said Tommy.

"Around, huh?" said Gaspar. "Hasn't Tommy become secretive? Well, enough small talk, then. It was fun. We should do it again sometime. But now –" He eyed Tommy. "You remember the pertinent question, right, Tommy?"

Tommy glanced down at his hands, still in his pockets. "I have money."

"The price has gone up."

Tommy looked at a thousand windows fronting the street, all watching him. "Doesn't matter."

Gaspar backed two quiet steps further into the alley, withdrawing his smile. What shadows there were, Gaspar found. Tommy followed him as if magnetized. Gaspar's voice dropped into an all-business whisper. "I've got the cure for the Cure, now, Tommy, if you want."

He slipped a tiny, clear plastic vial from inside his jacket and rocked it back and forth slowly in front of Tommy's face. "Special stuff, cut with anti-Cure additives." Deep violet liquid swayed inside the vial like a jeweled level. "A hit a day keeps the Cure away."

Tommy stared at the vial, radiating heat without light. Tommy's veins gaped with desire. He leaned forward into its warmth.

He slid his hands from his pockets, fists clutching crumpled ones and fives, but with enough tens and twenties to make Gaspar's eyes dilate.

Then his grin shrank, millimeter by millimeter. "Now, Tommy, my close personal friend, you wouldn't be trying to con a con-man?" The vial disappeared back inside the track suit. "You wouldn't be trying to set me up, now, would you?" Gaspar's left hand slid around to the small of his back, exactly where a pistol might be holstered.

"No." Tommy held out his hands. "I have money."

"Yes, you do, don't you?" said Gaspar. His smile crawled out from under a rock. "And how is that? You show up out of nowhere, unaccountably alive with fistfuls of cash after six months of junkie genocide. 'Around' seems to have been a very prosperous place for you. What's an honest man like myself to think of something so – so convenient, Tommy?"

"But –"

"They want me dead, Tommy. Dead for selling anti-cure ezy, or for not selling enough, or maybe for something completely different. I don't know."

"They?"

"They?" Gaspar mimicked Tommy's confusion and giggled. "Come on, Tommy. You know who they are. After all, you're their errand boy, aren't you? My sixth sense rattles and hums like a speaker waiting to pick up the first feedback of conspiracy coming too close, and I think you're it, Tommy, my wretched, drug-addled, chemical-ruined husk of a friend. They do have a sense of irony, using poor, harmless, slack-jawed, drooling Tommy-boy to set me up, but did they really think a cheap Manchurian junkie was going to fool me?" A revolver appeared in Gaspar's hand.

Tommy barely noticed. He stared at Gaspar's chest. The vial still radiated warmth, even out of sight. A cold tremor shook his body. "But – I need it."

Gaspar giggled. "But I don't need you, Tommy." He cocked the revolver's hammer. "Go back to Manchuria. Tell them you no speakee the lingo no more."

"Here." Tommy's voice cracked. He unclenched his fingers. Bills fluttered to the pavement like a magician's hands. "Take it."

Gaspar's eyes followed the money down, the muzzle dipping

with his gaze.

The vial whispered promises. Tommy figured they were lies, but he didn't care. He grabbed Gaspar's gun-hand and twisted it with a crack like crumpled paper. The bones of Gaspar's wrist collapsed under the weight of desperation and just the right lucky leverage.

The gunshot that followed wasn't even as loud as the bones breaking.

Gaspar sagged against the wall. Tommy still held the gun, Gaspar's hand twisted around backwards on the grip like it was half unscrewed. Tommy let go. Gaspar slid to the ground.

"No," sighed Tommy. He knelt, fast and hard enough to crack his knees on the pavement. He tore at Gaspar's jacket, unable to even work the zipper, until the fabric ripped wide. Gaspar bled, a rhythmic burble of blood regurgitating from a hole the size of a pinkie ring in his chest. "No, no, no, please god, no, don't let –"

But the vial was intact. Tommy cradled it in both hands as he stood.

Gaspar said something, a plea or threat, but Tommy turned his back and shuffled away. He shoved his hand in his pocket, enclosing the vial. He stopped at the red light on the corner, his back to the drugstore.

The smell of wet fur seeped out from between the nails and plywood, enveloping him.

He held his breath. He didn't turn around. He was safe now – no shadow doctors could steal his warmth with cold scalpels. Just holding the vial warmed him. He had no need to look inside the store, no need to see what he already knew was there.

But no amount of boards and nails – or even time – could stop the stench from switch-backing up from his hypothalamus to his frontal lobes. He remembered why he had tried to quit in the first place. He remembered –

*　*　*　*　*

– the smell of cheap scented candles, some artificial woodsy scent like a forest had been freshly painted with the cheapest paint available.

Tommy sat on a swaybacked couch salvaged from an alley, right on top of its last surviving spring, his tail-bone balanced tip to tip on its mirror-image in the cushion. The candles didn't quite illuminate the darkness in the room. Their scent didn't quite cover the urine.

"Tico's gone," said Tommy. "So's Henry. So's Wayne."

"Brain-dead dumbfucks," said Aldo, standing in the doorway. He had a weightlifter's chest, hairy arms and chicken legs. He had black eyes and long, uneven, black hair and beard. "They got lost. Fell in the shitter. Who knows? Dumbfucks."

"They're gone, Aldo. Disappeared. They –"

"No!" said Aldo. He flopped onto the couch with a squeak. "No dumbfucks tonight. Dumbfucks are a downer. Dumbfucks are –" He groped for a word. "Dumb," he finally said, and he laughed.

"I've been hearing – stories," said Tommy. He didn't look at Aldo when he said it. When he did look, Aldo stared at him.

"Dumbfuck!" Aldo tried to laugh, but couldn't. "Stories's jus' stories. Boogeymen. Ooowooowooo," he wailed, halfway between a plastered ghost and the squashed siren of a wrecked French police car. He waved his hands back and forth in front of Tommy's face. "Scary boogeymen stories." He took his eyes away from Tommy and slid a vial of ezy out of his jeans. He set it on the table in front of the couch with a tiny click.

Tommy tried to think about Tico, about Henry and Wayne, but couldn't. He watched Aldo instead.

Rain slashed the windowpanes like glass-cutters. A lightning flash overpowered the candles.

"I'm quitting," said Tommy.

"Then why're you here?" said Aldo. He passed the vial back and forth over the candle, the flame dipping and ducking under his thumb. He didn't flinch.

Tommy knew Aldo was coming down, because he could talk. "I'm quitting," he said again.

"Then quit already," said Aldo. He tried to shrug, like a tremor or a spasm rippling through his shoulders, as if the part of his brain that controlled those muscles had long since been eroded by ezy. "That much more for me." He pushed a hypodermic needle into the vial on his third try.

Tommy salivated. Ezy distilled itself into a Gauguin or a Rembrandt or a Pollack, or all three rolled up and injected straight into his bloodstream – all the color, the emotion, the light, the chaos; all the talent and turbulence, the inference and darkness; the raw, primordial, oozing, overpowering quicksand vision that closed over his head and squeezed his eyes and ears until they hurt. Tommy thought he remembered that he had been an art student at some point in the past.

Aldo touched the tip of the needle to his skin. A drop of ezy popped and spread over the center of the tattoo of a bulls-eye on the inside of his left forearm.

Tommy could feel the warm steel point of the needle, even from the other end the couch. "Isn't that too much?" he said, but he didn't even take himself seriously.

Aldo pushed the needle into his arm through a swelling bead of blood and thumbed the plunger down. He closed his eyes. His mouth opened. "Toomushnev'r'nuf," he slurred a few seconds later.

Tommy thought he could see Aldo's tongue swell, pushing itself out of his mouth.

Aldo sagged back, needle still bobbing in his arm. His head lolled onto the couch's arm-rest. Sweat pockmarked his forehead and darkened the underarms of his t-shirt. He smiled with his mouth wide open. "Ooowooowooo," he droned. He jerked his arms around until they tangled and dropped to the cushion. "Ooowooo big bad boo-eyman." He laughed. "Hairy stories, jus' hairy." His smile melted into drool.

"I'm quitting," said Tommy.

Aldo slitted his eyes at Tommy. He hauled himself upright. "'Umfu'." His tongue lolled. His gaze slid off Tommy's face.

"What?" said Tommy.

Aldo stared over Tommy's shoulder at the window. His eyes dilated wide as smudged fingerprints, as if his hallucination were pressing its thumbs into his eyes. "Oh," he said. "Boo-eyman."

"What?"

Lightning flashed a huge shadow into the room. Glass shattered and crashed against Tommy's back, cutting his neck. He winced, hunched over. Meat-cleaver pieces broke into switchblade shards on the floor. Rain and wind snuffed the candles.

The shadow came through the window. The floor trembled

as it touched down, somewhere just out of the corner of Tommy's left eye. The couch bounced.

Tommy cringed. SWAT, he thought. A black figure in body armor, ski mask and boots; but then the stink hit him. Like being smothered in the sodden fur of a wet dog.

The shadow passed him. Holding something in its right hand. A night-stick? Tommy wasn't sure, but something white flashed past his face, then connected with Aldo.

Aldo's throat exploded in a spray of blood like a shattered ruby glittering in a flash of lightning.

Tommy stomped his eyes closed. Not a night-stick. He froze. He heard Aldo's blood splatter across the wall with a hissing sound like air from a slashed tire. Fur had covered the cop, and he was the size of a gorilla, with one huge arm that hung to his knees. Not a cop.

Tommy heard a low whistle each time the arm slashed down onto Aldo – a wet slap, slap, slap like a pig being hacked with a machete. Aldo snorted and snuffled, finally stopped. But the slashes still carved the air; jet-streams fluttered Tommy's hair, cooled his face. Blood speckled his cheek.

The couch lurched under the blows, the slap-slap sliding into a single thud as wood cracked, collapsed and slumped. Tommy started to topple towards Aldo, towards the shadow. He curled into a ball, clutched his knees to his chest, rolled to his left, away from Aldo, from the shadow, just away. He pissed himself, soaked his pants, until he and the cushion were both sodden. He felt a weight thump against his leg and lay there.

Then – he heard feeding sounds.

Tommy's skin crawled. Adrenaline goaded him to run, to jump through the broken window, to do – anything, something – but he forced himself to freeze. His heart jerked at its leash.

He tried not to listen.

And then – everything stopped.

Tommy inhaled, slowly, through his mouth.

It moved. The cushion sagged under its weight, the fabric pulling against Tommy's butt. The couch swayed and creaked, first to his right, then his left, as the beast spidered its way closer to him.

Bristles scratched Tommy's cheek like steel wool. Tommy shivered. Its heat swabbed his face. Tommy stopped breathing.

He didn't hear it breathe at all.

Then tiny, cold, wormlike corkscrews of its tongue swirled across his face, connecting the dots of Aldo's blood.

I'll quit, I'll quit, I'll quit – Tommy's thoughts shone with adrenaline – just please god don't let it kill me, please, please, I'll quit, I swear I'll quit, I'll never touch the stuff again, please, god, please.

It pulled back.

Tommy waited for the claw-hand, waited for it to rip his throat out, to tear his belly open. Waited as if one second – impossibly, inconceivably – was not going to be followed by another second.

He couldn't open his eyes. Couldn't look at it. He pressed his face into his knees, breathed the stink of his own piss to cut the smell of wet fur.

Waited.

Silence drowned the house.

The cushion and his pants grew cold. He shivered in the air blowing through the broken window.

And nothing happened.

He slowly felt like he was being born into a bright, clean, second-chance world. He laughed – couldn't help himself – shut his mouth. The dried saliva cracked on his cheeks.

But nothing happened.

He opened his eyes.

Blood clotted the walls, dripped from the ceiling. Tongue-tracks smeared the red like finger-paint.

Aldo – what was left of Aldo – oozed into the couch through a sieve of sheared ribs, his chest pried open into a bowl of mush. He looked – surprised.

Aldo's left arm – pulled out by its roots – lay against Tommy's legs. A cold tremor shook him. The needle, still stuck in Aldo's empty vein, quivered in sympathy.

Tommy had the answer to his prayer.

*   *   *   *   *

Tommy threw off the blanket after the cockroaches were gone, the wool rustling like steam. The vial radiated heat throughout the studio apartment, burned the sweat out of him, burned everything out of him but the need.

The Cure scrabbled in circles in the shadows, turned itself inside-out in anticipation.

Tommy froze. He wasn't going to use the vial. He'd only gotten it for comfort. Nothing more. He'd intended to throw it out when he woke up. He had just planned on sleeping for awhile. To get his strength back. To get warm. That was all.

He climbed out of bed. His muscles bubbled on his skeleton, burning like tendrils of hot wax creeping along his bones.

The Cure withdrew its white talon into the darkness, cocking to swing.

Tommy's muscles surged toward the vial on their own; he couldn't stop himself.

It's safe this time, he thought. It's safe.

He cried as he picked up the hypo. Snot dripped from his nose; he sucked it back in. It's safe. The needle trembled in his fingers like a red-lined speedometer. It's safe.

He stuck himself in the finger twice before he got the needle into the vial. He couldn't stop himself. A spasm shook his body, jerking the needle out, the hypo full.

He found a vein easy, like a plug in a socket. The tip of the needle tickled his bloodstream. Fear began to dissolve. He thumbed the plunger down –

– a liquid, sunlit, Flash Gordon, chrome-plated, jet-stream rush –

– but the plunger didn't stop. It left his thumb and sank slowly, by itself, through the reservoir and then through the bulging needle straight into his vein, leaving a straight, open path from his blood through the hollow dangling needle, through the empty reservoir, out into the air like a gaping mouth.

Dust motes began to swirl around the syringe – circling red, green, white in the changing neon – a glittering carousel of air being sucked into his arm.

A couple of dollar bills fluttered on the table, then flew into his arm. His arm vacuumed up a dime, a penny, a quarter, a plastic fork and knife, a pizza box, a flying snake of ashes from the ashtray, cigarettes, matches. The abyss inside him sucked the table clean.

And then the table itself, the legs collapsing clack, clack, clack, clack, all swirling like a molten candy cane into his arm, and then a pillow, blankets and mattress rushed into him, and the sink wrenched itself out of the wall, and paint stripped itself free in huge sheets and flapped across the room like beige ghosts. Nails creaked out of their holes; electricity arced out of sockets; and then the apartments around him, the people screaming like Doppler shifts as they were pulled inside, the cars outside, the streets breaking into chunks, the city, the life and the darkness and the energy and the stars and everything and everything –

– except the Cure, still waiting in the absence of light around him, two eyes still shining as if they were polished, darker than the dark void that was all that remained.

Tommy felt his skin press in on his ribs, sag into the hollow of his still-empty belly. Ezy wasn't enough. Everything wasn't enough.

The Cure lurched off its haunches. It slashed Tommy's throat, but the talons, honed and hard, skittered off his skin, throwing a shower of sparks instead of blood. It slashed again, like a pitchfork scraping armor.

Tommy grabbed its arm before the third slash. Clutched its wrist. Squeeeeeezed. Felt its bones slide and twist around themselves inside his grip.

It pulled, twisted, but couldn't free itself. It heaved itself backwards, but went nowhere.

Tommy just squeezed harder. Bones splintered. Tommy's muscles felt strong as rigor mortis. His skin hardened like a thousand layers of lacquer, shiny and seamless, glowing a deep violet.

The Cure uncoiled its other arm – a thin, almost prehensile thing hidden in fur along its left side – and wrapped it around Tommy's neck, constricting, strangling. It didn't even dent Tommy's new skin.

Tommy yanked it from its socket and tossed it aside.

The Cure squirmed in his grip.

Tommy crushed its wrist, bent it backwards over itself and rammed its talons into its chest. Blood crept over his hand. He wrenched the talons back out, bone scraping past bone like a fire-ax twisting out of a gash in a Dumpster.

The Cure sagged.

Blood bubbled from the triple-wound, and Tommy knew what he was hungry for. He slammed the talons back into the Cure and sawed its torso open from neck to crotch. He buried his face in the wound, drinking its stolen blood.

Sweet. Sticky. The more he drank, the more he wanted. He sucked the blood that pooled, squeezed its heart like a sponge over his open mouth, licked bones dry. And then he dropped the corpse. He slurped the last few drops of blood from his own fingers.

He stared at his hands, the skin deep violet and smooth, without even fingerprints. Not human skin. Not Tommy's skin.

He realized all at once that the rumors had been true, his own visions of secret surgeries and alien abduction real. The Cure was branching out from addicts to drugstores; and, in response, the deep-black government doctors had strapped him to a table beneath glaring lights and inserted the desire to kill, transforming him into an anti-Cure binary weapon – Gaspar's special ezy activating the experiments, activating the additions to his body and the subtractions to his humanity.

He stood in his apartment, alone in the silence with a corpse. There was no blood. His deep violet, invulnerable skin glistened like polished night, absorbing the changing neon.

He could smell more of the creatures, out there, all over the city, stalking addicts. Urges surged up from his hindbrain, lighting off arcs of neurons like verbs: Hunt – Kill – Feed.

He felt transformed, mind and body, into a killer, a savior of society, a Cure for the Cure.

For a moment he wondered what would happen when he had killed the last Cure.

But only for a moment.

His violet skin slowly faded. His belly whined for more blood. He salivated from the beautiful scent of wet fur saturating the air.

It smelled like food.

BABIES IS SMART

Babies is smart. I'm here in jail right now because babies is smarter than you think, and that's all I got to say on the subject.

Except this –

Babies is sneaky little bastards, too, always being all baby-cute and goo-goo-happy all the while they're figuring ways to screw you. You gotta watch 'em all the time, every second, otherwise they'll have your watch or your wallet or they'll lock you in a goddamn closet just like that, and believe me, I know it for a fact, because I've been there, done that. Goddamn babies.

And they drool too. Drool and puke and shit and piss. All babies is good for is making things wet. Goddamn babies. Always getting everybody else to wipe up their piss and puke so they don't have to do for themselves. How sweet is that? Like they're some kind of high and mighty royalty, and every morning Janice has to leave just because she's got to go to work, and, since I'm currently between jobs, all of a sudden I'm stuck mopping up various baby bodily fluids like I'm not smart enough to do anything else.

I want you to know this was all Janice's fault. She knew better than to leave me with a goddamn baby, especially one that ain't even mine. What'd she expect was gonna happen except what did happen? She knows I don't take no shit from no one. But just because babies is smart doesn't mean their mothers gotta be smart too, I guess.

Goddamn Janice.

Goddamn babies.

So the baby started screaming to high heaven with its baby police-siren voice. It screamed before Janice left; it screamed while she headed out the door, and it screamed for the next three hours solid while I was trying to watch TV. Screamed non-stop. Never shut up. Scream, scream, scream. And what the hell did it have to scream about anyway? I'm the one who has to smell it and wipe up all its goddamn leaking fluids, not the other way around. Goddamn baby.

So I went over to its crib.

"OK, baby," I said, "now it's just you and me. No Momma, no Daddy, no nobody but you and me. So I'm only gonna say this once. Shut your fucking pie-hole, you goddamn baby!"

But did it listen? Hell, no. It screamed louder. And you know what else it did? It smiled. That goddamn baby smiled at me. It knew what it was doing. Gas, my skinny white ass. It knew exactly what it was doing. Like I said – babies is smart.

Screaming and smiling. Making fun of me, is what it was doing, like when I used to get made fun of at the paint-store job, with my boss and customers yelling and complaining at me and yammering non-stop like each one of 'em had a pair of pliers clamped onto my ear and they all just squeezed and twisted until my brain started to bleed into my eyes, before I finally got smart and quit.

Goddamn jobs.

Goddamn Janice.

Goddamn babies.

So, to make a long story short, it was still screaming. Now, I coulda cooed and gurgled over it like Janice does all the time, because that's what it says to do in her baby-books that she gets out of the library, except it never makes no never mind. Baby still screams. So I know to do something different.

So I leaned over and got right in its cherry-red, scrunched-up, screaming baby face, an inch away tops, and I screamed too: "Shut up! Shut up! Shut the fuck UP! Aaaaaaaaaaaaaah! AAAAAAAAAAAAAAAAAAH!"

It screamed and I screamed right back at it until I scraped my voice raw and my spit flew into its face. See how it likes someone else leaking bodily fluids for a change.

Now, I know what you're thinking. You're thinking, that ain't no way to talk to a baby, but I was just showing it that I could make just as much racket as it could, be just as goddamn unreasonable, and that it wasn't the center of the goddamn universe. And also, by the way, that I wasn't gonna take no shit, not from any customers, not from any boss, and sure as shit not from any goddamn baby. I was in charge, not the baby, so I screamed at it like we was both babies, only I was the bigger one.

But did it stop its screaming? Hell, no. It screamed louder.

So I picked that baby up. "Oh, little baby," I said, "don't scream and cry like a goddamn whore that didn't get paid." And then I grabbed it by the ankles. "Or else," I said. And I swung it in a great big arc over my head and smashed its head down just as hard as I could on the radiator.

SPONG!

Oh, that sound! That sound its head made when it hit the radiator was like no other sound I'd ever heard before. That sound shivered through me like I'd just shot my load into the mouth of the best hooker I'd ever seen, and, believe me, I've been there, done that.

I sprang up hard in my drawers like an aluminum baseball bat, harder than Janice had ever made me. I damn near fell over, like all my bones had turned into electricity, sparking and skittering around inside me. I felt like I shimmered, like that baby jerked the breath out of me, strapped my heart into a paint-mixing machine and shook it just this side of dying.

Except that's not quite right, know what I mean? It's hard to explain just how that sound felt.

Maybe it was like some of that baby-innocence spilled out of it and slopped onto me like I was cement and it was 100% pure spring water from a bottle, and for maybe a millionth of a second I had potential, like my parole officer is always yammering on about. Maybe I finally understood what he meant. I had potential, like I could've flowed into any shape in the world I wanted, been anyone, done anything. Maybe I felt like everything I'd ever wanted and hoped for was suddenly right there in front of me, the best feeling I'd ever had, ever could have, right there –

– and then my millionth of a second ended, and I flopped back into being just me in a room dangling a goddamn baby by the ankles again, with nothing special added, like the baby-innocence had disappeared and my head hardened back into a chunk of concrete.

That goddamn baby had just showed it to me, showed me what life could be like, what I was missing, just passed the best feeling in the world in front of my eyes, teased me with it and then took it away. Making fun of me.

I guess it was right about then that I lost my temper, so I figured to myself – why the hell not? So I proceeded to windmill that baby against the radiator like I was doing speedballs and PCP both in unreasonable amounts, and believe me, I've been there, done that.

SPONG!

SPONG!

SPONG!

Because I knew – I just goddamn knew – that that baby had the secret to life and happiness and who knew what the hell else locked up inside its goddamn baby-head, and I wanted that feeling again. So I kept cranking it into the radiator.

SPONG!

SPONG!

SPONG!

That sound gushed through the radiator and into the pipes and through the walls like blood, and my swinging hand was the heartbeat.

SPONG!

SPONG!

SPONG!

That sound reverberated faster and faster like I was turbocharged on potential, like my very own heart beating into the world, and I was it – I was it, baby – the middle of everything, the warm meaty sparking sizzle of life itself transferring itself from me to the world through the meeting of that baby and that radiator.

And as the electricity shivered in the tip of my cock, I figured I finally knew why people had goddamn babies in the first place. And believe me, there'd be a lot less stealing and drinking and cheating on wives in the world if there were more baby-clanging going on. But I can see that you don't agree with me on that sentiment. That's OK – everybody's entitled to his own opinion.

But then you know what happened? The sound changed. Now, you gotta realize, at this point I still didn't fully understand what a brainy evil little fucker that baby was. I mean, the first thing I figured was that the sound had changed because its little head had gone soft with the repeated clanging, or maybe all the blood leaking out of it had changed the pitch or something, but then I realized that it was faking. Because there was just no way there could be that much blood inside ten babies, much less just one, and a scrawny, undersized, runty one like it is. There just couldn't be that much blood, because blood slopped and sloshed around everywhere in the living room like some goddamn baby-graffiti splattering the walls and ceiling and floor and windows and couch and carpet and just everyplace until I even felt it squishing between my toes and dripping off the tip of my nose, not to mention the tip of my hard-on, like I had thrashed a million-gallon can of vermilion-sunset satin-finish paint all over the place, and if babies had that much blood, then they'd be nothing but blood, and then some, and I know they got other shit inside them, like shit and drool and stomach contents and stuff.

So I knew all the blood wasn't real, just some kind of deceiving baby-trick like squid ink to make me think I'd hurt it real bad and make me less mad, but of course that only made me more mad.

Goddamn fake baby-blood.

And then I guess I sort of lost my grip on the little sonuvabitch, what with all the greasy fake blood all over everything, and I sailed that baby clear across the room, and its head stove in a part of the wall like a shot-put, so don't try and tell me that its head wasn't harder than wallboard. And poop shot out of its diapers like it was a shit-powered rocket-ship, and the whole room smelled like my face had gotten shoved nose-deep into a goddamn dirty baby-crack. No exaggeration.

Now, you can see that there was a lull at this point. Sure, I was still mad, but there was a lull, and maybe that would've been the end of it – baby tried its baby-tricks, and I bashed it around a little, but no harm done, no foul – except that baby wouldn't let it go. So the way I see it, everything from that point on was the baby's fault.

It hit the floor and tried to roll under the couch, and as it rolled over, I could see that it was still smiling. Smiling and giggling, because it figured it was smarter than me, and when Janice got home and saw all the blood, she would blame me and not the baby.

So I got mad all over again and grabbed the little fucker before it could skitter away under the furniture like a cockroach, and I shook it good like it was in the paint-mixing machine, all the while screaming, you ain't so smart! You ain't so fucking smart! And its head snapped around all back and forth and sideways like a bobble-headed vampire trying to sink its powerful pointy little baby-teeth into me, and goddamn it if its mouth didn't just drop right open into a red, lopsided grin, mocking me, like I couldn't even begin to conceive of what a cunning evil genius it was.

So I jerked it up high over my head to smash it on the coffee table, but I guess I forgot about the ceiling fan, because the spinning blades just sucked that baby right outta my hands like explosive decompression, and it spun around and around a couple of times, and I don't think you'll be amazed when I tell you that that goddamn baby was still smiling ear-to-ear around that fan-blade chomped in its mouth, and then it slipped off the fan with a sound like yanking a machete out of a dead dog, and that was a good sound, like always, but not quite as good as the radiator sound. And it shot across the room again right at the window, hosing blood everywhere until it hit the window and just crashed right through the glass. Like shit through a goose, I swear to God. No exaggeration.

And then, I guess, time sort of stopped.

That goddamn baby just hung there, four floors up, in mid-air, and everything stopped. Felt like a minute at least. I remember seeing a piece of glass stuck right between its eyes as it stared at me staring at it.

And I swear to God it smiled at me with its gaping red hacked-out maw of a smile. It just wouldn't goddamn die. That baby took everything I handed out and could've taken more, like it had some kind of super-protective baby-genes or something.

And then a crow flew past and pecked once at its head, and it fell, and a second later I heard SPLAT from the street, and that was a good sound, but not a great one, and then screeching tires and women wailing and horns honking and police sirens, and it couldn't have been more than a couple of minutes later that you cops came barreling through the door, and, well, you already know the story from that point on.

So, in conclusion, all I got to say is this:

"Dead?" Hell. "Murdered?" My ass! That baby ain't murdered or dead. I know you got it stashed here somewhere in the station. I can still hear it screaming. My skull is buzzing with it at this very moment like a Magic Fingers motel bed. Asleep. Awake. Don't matter. I can hear it. Screaming never stops.

Goddamn baby.

John Everson is the author of the erotic horror novelette Failure *(Delirium Books, 2006) and the Bram Stoker Award-winning occult horror novel* Covenant *(Delirium Books, 2004).* Sacrifice, *a sequel to* Covenant, *will be released early in 2007. Everson is also the author of three horror and dark fantasy short story collections –* Needles & Sins *(Necro Publications, 2007),* Vigilantes of Love *(Twilight Tales, 2003) and* Cage of Bones & Other Deadly Obsessions *(Delirium Books, 2000).*

His short fiction has appeared in magazines like Space and Time, Wicked Karnival, Red Scream, Black October *and* Grue, *and in the anthologies* Damned: An Anthology of the Lost, Cold Flesh, Small Bites, Spooks! *and more. His short story "Pumpkin Head," which appears in this collection, is one of his most popular stories, having previously appeared in two magazines and a hardcover collection. It is currently being translated into French for foreign publication.*

John lives in the west suburbs of Chicago with his wife Geri, son Shaun and evil, domineering writing companion, Kiwi the cockatoo. For more info, art, music and fiction, visit John Everson: Dark Arts at www.johneverson.com.

MAXIMUM LOADING LEVEL

John
Everson

THE WHITE HOUSE

"There is no poetry in death," Mrs. Tanser said. "Only loss and rot, stink and waste. I never could understand those gothic romantics who celebrate the dark and lust after the cycle of decay."

The little girl in front of her didn't say a thing, but nodded creamy, unblemished cheeks as if she understood.

"I suppose that doesn't make much sense to you," Mrs. Tanser continued, running a powder-coated finger up the girl's cheek. "You came here hoping to sell cookies and to visit my nieces, and here I am talking to you about death! But I can't deny death, mind you. Everything has its place. And every place, its thing."

The older woman laughed, and stood up from the table. Her plate of thinly sliced apples remained untouched, uneaten, the brown creep of time already shadowing the fruit. The girl's plate, however glistened with the juice of apple long gone.

Mrs. Tanser ground a pestle into a tall bucket that squeaked and shifted on the counter as she worked.

"Well, I'm sorry my nieces Genna and Jillie aren't here any longer. They only came for a visit, so I'm glad you got to meet them. Perhaps you'll have the chance to be with them again soon. But I talk too much and time passes. Too fast, too fast. Eat my apples dear. Waste not, want not."

The plate slid across the table. Mrs. Tanser raised a silver eyebrow as it did.

"You are afraid of this house, aren't you?"

The child nodded, slowly. Her eyes were blue and wide, and the reflection of the older woman's methodic grinding and pummeling of the substance in the bucket glimmered like a ghost in their mirror.

"I can't say that I'm surprised. Quite the reputation it has. I didn't realize that when I moved in, but now it makes sense what a steal it was. I knew there was something wrong when the realtor quoted me the price – you could see it in her face. She was afraid, that silly woman was, not that she knew why. A beautiful old mansion like this, perched on the top of the most scenic hill in town? I have to admit, I didn't care what was wrong with it – for that price, I thought, I could fix it. And then I moved in, and started teaching down at Barnard Elementary, and I found out why that girl was scared. You know, she wouldn't even walk into the house past the front foyer?"

Mrs. Tanser laughed. The pestle clinked against the top of the bucket, and a hazy cloud puffed from the opening like blown flour.

"The one warning that woman said to me was, 'You know, it's a bad place for children.' I didn't even ask why. 'I don't have any,' I told her. That shut her up. Or maybe it didn't, I didn't care. I walked up those gorgeous oak stairs that wind out of the living room and up to the boudoir. I wanted to see it all, with or without her help. She didn't come with me."

Mrs. Tanser stopped her grinding and considered. "Would you like to see the upstairs?" she asked.

The little girl shrugged, and the older woman dropped the pestle.

"That settles it. Genna and Jillie aren't here, but I can still show you the house. Come on upstairs. I'm going to show you the most beautiful four-poster bed your little eyes have ever seen. The girls loved it! It may be the only four-poster bed your little eyes have ever seen."

The girl rose from the table, hands held straight at the sides of her red and green striped skirt. She wanted to leave, felt embarrassed that she'd been coaxed into staying somehow. Her freckles threatened to burst into flame as she waited for Mrs. Tanser to wash her hands in the sink.

"C'mon then," Mrs. Tanser said at last, and led the girl back towards the front door she'd come in. Her backpack from school still lay abandoned on the floor nearby. Mrs. Tanser put a foot on the first varnished step, and then paused.

"What's your name again then, young lady?"

"Tricia," the girl answered, in a voice high as a flute song.

"Tricia," Mrs. Tanser announced, waving at the crystal jewels of the chandelier above, and the burnished curves of the banister on the second floor landing above.

"Welcome to White House," she said. "Welcome to the House of Bones."

At the top of the landing, Mrs. Tanser stopped again. "This house was built in 1878 by Garfield White," she announced. "I looked it up. He was a railroad man, made his living helping folks move their steel and wood and food and such from one place to the next. Why he settled here, in the middle of nowhere, I'll never know, but there you go. Every thing has a place, and every place a thing. He built this place, and put his wife here in it to raise their son. Maybe he thought she'd give the boy a good upbringing here, away from the corruption and sin of the cities."

Mrs. Tanser motioned the girl to follow her down the hall to the dark rimmed doorway of a room.

"That woman spent her time in here, so the stories go, day after day after day while her Garfield rode the rails making his fortune. He stayed out on those rails more and more, hoping maybe to gain his son an inheritance."

The older woman stepped with a click and an echoey clack into the room. The walls were papered in a pattern of whirling pinks and blossomed yellows. But the garish sidelights did little to detract from the majesty of the enormous mahoghany bed that dominated the center. Its rich posts rose from lion claw paws on the floor to taper in spears to within inches of the faded ceiling. A translucent gauze of yellowed lace hung between the posts and darkened the space with ghostly light.

"The more her husband stayed lost on the trains, the more his wife stayed lost here, in this very bed," Mrs. Tanser said.

"Go ahead, sit on it yourself and see why!"

Tricia stepped into the room but stopped at the edge of the mattress, which was nearly as tall as her.

"Use the step," Mrs. Tanser said, pointing to the dark wooden box near the girl's feet. "In those days, you wanted to sleep as high above the ground as you could. Rats, you know."

Tricia hopped up on the step with the mention of rodents, and rolled her body onto the heavy down mattress, smiling at the caress of the silken blue comforter that covered it.

"They called it the White House, and not because it was in Washington, D.C.," Mrs. Tanser said. "But it was anything but white inside. Mrs. White kept all of the drapes pulled shut, and spent more and more time here, in this bed. They say she was trying to make it feel like nighttime inside, so her son would sleep. Had the collick, and cried all day long. But pulling the drapes did nothing to calm the boy, and after awhile, Mrs. White went a little bit mad, I think. Day after day, night after night, her baby cried, cried, cried and she paced this floor with him, pounding his tiny back and begging him to burp and then screaming at him to burp."

Mrs. Tanser shook her head.

"That boy never saw that nest egg his father was out putting away. When Mr. White came back from one of his long trips down the rails, he found the house dark, and all the shutters pulled. I probably shouldn't be telling you this, you being a young girl and all – but you've probably seen worse on TV. Oh the things they show on that tube." Mrs. Tanser shook her head, brows creased in dreadful sadness.

"When Mr. White came home that day, he walked up those same stairs you and I just did, and knew right away something was wrong. I won't say more than this, but the smell was in the air, and he was no fool. He rushed to the bedroom and threw open this door and…"

Tricia's eyes widened as the story unfolded.

"…when the light streamed into the pitch-black room, he found his wife and his son, here in the shadows. Only they were in no condition to leave. The poor boy was hung from his tiny neck right off of that pole there," Mrs. Tanser pointed at the right pole at the foot of the bed. "Mrs. White had tried to quiet him by wrapping a sheet around his head – but when he didn't quiet, she'd finally snapped. She hung him by his tiny neck like a Christmas ornament at the foot of the bed, and when he finally quieted, she laid down on the pillow and went to sleep. When she woke, and realized what she'd done, she took her own life, using her husband's straight razor.

"If I took the sheets off this bed you could still see the marks of her blood. Nobody's ever changed that mattress. She laid down right there, where you are, and cut her self again and again and again until she couldn't cut or scream anymore."

Tricia leapt from the bed as if it had turned to a stove burner.

Mrs. Tanser grinned, wrinkles catching at the corner of her eyes like broken glass.

"She used that blade so much, they say she had to have a closed casket. Can't imagine cutting your own face with a razor-blade myself, but, I can't imagine hanging your own baby, neither!

"There's a reason they started calling this place the House of Bones. But that came later. Mr. White kept this place for almost 30 years after his wife killed their son, and herself here. And he never remarried. In fact, he may have been dead for a year or more before the town grew the wiser. He was gone for long periods at a time on the railroad, and it was only when the spring winds brought a tree down on the west wing of the house that someone from the town realized it had been months and months since Mr. White had been seen. When they looked into it, they found out that he hadn't been out on a rail for more than a year, and that's when someone thought to look in the basement."

Mrs. Tanser looked at the trembling girl and shook her head.

"I'm sorry, I'm scaring you. My home does not have a cheery history, I must admit. But it's fascinating too, don't you think?"

The old woman shook her head. "C'mon downstairs, and I'll buy some of those Girl Scout cookies. A lady needs her vices, huh?"

✦   ✦   ✦   ✦   ✦

The doorbell rang. But there was no silhouette showing through the stained purple glass in the front door of White House.

Mrs. Tanser answered the ring, nevertheless, and smiled as she saw the pale features of the girl on the landing, shivering and yet waiting outside. So small, she couldn't even send her shadow through the glass.

"Come in child," she insisted. "You'll catch your death of cold. I don't believe your mother lets you go out like that in the fall chill."

Tricia entered the house again, driven by a feeling she could not have explained. The house scared her to death. Mrs. Tanser was strange. But interesting. A welcome diversion after a boring day at school.

"I didn't think you'd come back after the story of Mr. and Mrs. White," the teacher exclaimed. "Sometimes I feel like I am just the steward for this house. I have to give its history, no matter how twisted it may be."

She motioned the girl into the kitchen, a room colored in orange walls and burnished counters.

"You're probably hoping for my nieces, but I'm afraid they're not around to play with you right now. Can I cut you an apple?" Mrs. Tanser asked again, and Tricia nodded.

"Good."

After awhile, the older woman went back to her grinding, pounding work at the counter, and talked to Tricia from across the room.

"Hmmm…where did we leave off last time? How it all began, I think. Yes. I suppose you're wondering, what happened after the Whites lived in White House?"

The girl nodded, and Mrs. Tanser barely waited for that response.

Mr. White was found in the basement. I won't go into how his disposition was, other than to say that the bones of Mrs. White and Baby White were found with him. The house was eventually sold to another family, and life went on – for a time."

Mrs. Tanser brushed the dust from the lapels of her maroon collar. It smeared like dried milk across her chest.

"You can't hide the past," she said. "Nor can you hide *from* the past. What is, *is*, and what was, *was*. The next people who bought this house pretended that the Whites hadn't killed themselves here, and as a result…"

Tricia looked up from her slice of apple with a keen gaze of expectation.

"Well, they didn't consider the fact that they might also spend their lives – and deaths – here."

"Sometimes," Mrs. Tanser said, eyes looking far, far away. "A mother's love is not endless. In fact, it doesn't even really begin."

The older woman rubbed a tear from the wrinkles at the side

of her eye, and forced a grin. "Silly old woman I am," she said. "You're just a girl and you can't even begin to understand the twists and cul de sacs of a mother's love. I had a tough one, is all, and even now I can hear her scolding me. I've met your mama at the PTA, and she's not like that. Not like that at all. You're a very lucky girl."

"So where was I? Oh yes, the next family. A pastor, the father was, come here all the way from Omaha. Why here, again I'll never know. This must be the end of the line for some folks, and they just don't know it. Hell, why would they come here if they did? Something draws them though, because no matter how many young folks try to escape this town after they graduate, the place keeps growing. Back in those days, before the Great War, there were just a couple hundred here, and the Martins moved into this house with a huge welcome from the townsfolk. For a time, Pastor Martin even held services right here in this house – in the sitting room I believe – until a proper parish chapel could be built down in the center of town."

"All that holiness didn't settle things apparently, though, in White House. Because the pastor and his family came to a similar end as the Whites' did. Things were happy here for a few years, and the Martins had two children, Becky and Joseph. But, just like Mr. White, Pastor Martin's vocation began to consume him, leaving Mrs. Martin here in the house all alone with the children day after day. The story goes, that Mrs. Martin got bit by the green bug, and started thinking that Pastor Martin was spending far too much time down at the new chapel in town. There's no telling if it's true or not, but she thought the pastor was making time with a pretty little hussy in the back pew, while she was trapped here, in this old, cold house with two screaming kids.

"I'm talking too big for you aren't I?" Mrs. Tanser said noting the confused expression on the girl's face. "The pastor's wife thought he had gotten a girlfriend, is the thing. And he was married to her and she didn't want him to have a girlfriend. So she locked little Becky and Joseph into a small room at the back of the house. Someone, probably Mr. White, had added on, and built the room by hand. It wasn't completely true. Sometimes, Pastor Martin would come home at night and hear those kids screaming in the back of the house, and when he'd let them out, they'd tumble into the house proper shaking and blue with cold, because none of the seams of that room were level. The outside could leech in easily; hell, you could see the grass waving in the wind through the gaps and the draughts on this hill in the winter are something horrible, I have to tell you. Even asleep in that big four-post bed upstairs, I put an afghan on top of the covers in December. Can you imagine how cold it must have been for those children when they could actually see the outside through the cracks in the walls?

"Anyway, Pastor Martin yelled at his wife many a time for how she treated those children, yelled so loud the people a mile down the hill in town could hear him and mark his words. And she'd yell right back, and accuse him of taking the Lord's work to the devil, not to mention that tart Beatrice Long. She thought he was making time with a church whore."

Tricia put a hand over her mouth to stifle a yawn, and Mrs. Tanser pushed the plate of apples closer to the girl.

"I'm going on too long, aren't I? Let me speed it up for you some. An old woman can go on. One day Pastor Martin came home and for once, the house was quiet. His wife told him the kids had gone to stay with friends in town for the weekend, and he heaved a sigh of relief. The noise had really begun to get to him, and that, as much as anything, was why he'd been spending more and more time at the chapel. The Martins reportedly had a lovely dinner, and even broke out a bottle of wine to celebrate their brief 'vacation' from the children. Pastor Martin tried to get romantic with his wife, but she waved him off of that. 'You wouldn't want to make more of the little screamers, would you?' she said."

Mrs. Tanser paused, looking quizzically at Tricia's moon-round cheeks. "That probably doesn't mean much to you yet, does it? Hmmm."

"Well, it came to Sunday, and Pastor Martin spoke after the church service with the folks his children were supposedly staying with, thanking them for their hospitality. But they looked confused at his thanks, and told him that they would be happy to have Becky and Joseph over any time, but they hadn't seen the kids these past few days.

"Pastor Martin was upset by that, and after the last service, headed home in a rush. He wondered if he'd gotten the family wrong that the kids were staying with. When he entered the house, for the third day in a row it was completely silent, but Mrs. Martin waited for him at the table.

"'Sit,' she insisted. 'Eat.'

"He sat, but asked her where the children were. Mrs. Martin smiled sweetly, and ignored him, fixing herself a sandwich and then pushing the plate towards him. 'Light or dark?' she asked.

"'Both,' he said absently, and as she put the meat on his plate, along with a long crust of bread, he asked her again. 'Where are the kids?'

"Mrs. Martin smiled that strange little grin again and nodded, as he lifted the bread to his mouth and chewed.

"'You're eating them dear. Becky's light, and Joseph's dark.'"

Tricia's eyes went wide and she set the piece of apple she held back on the plate, uneaten.

"Horrible, hmmm? Apparently Mrs. Martin had used that back room to turn her children into cold cuts. When he screamed and beat on her for her horrible crime, she only smiled and smiled, and told him to make more with Beatrice Long. Back then, in a town this size, they didn't have asylums, and so Mrs. Martin never actually left this house. Pastor Martin locked her in the room she'd killed her children in, and fed her meals at morning and night. She never came out of there again, and whenever he'd break down and cry and ask her 'why' all she would say was 'the house needs strong bones.'"

Mrs. Tanser grinned. "Creepy, hmm? Want to see the room?"

Tricia's eyes widened.

"Oh don't worry, the Martin's are long gone from there. Come along, I'll show you."

Mrs. Tanser led Tricia through a hallway and a long, dark sitting room to a white door. She turned a latch and a metal bolt clacked audibly before she turned the old round knob.

They stepped through into a small, dark room. It had no windows at all, but still was lit. The sun beamed in through hairline cracks in the grout between the stones that had been shaved and stacked to form the addition. Shadows played like anxious ghosts on the walls and dust motes rained in lazy dances as the wind shifted and groaned outside.

"This is it," Mrs. Tanser said. "The infamous White room. They think that Mr. White built it with his own hands, and used the bones of his wife and son as the grout between the rocks. Mrs. Martin followed his lead. The paint you see in here? The reason the room is so white? She ground up the bones of those two kids after carving them up for lunchmeat here in this room. She used the dust of their bones to paint this room an everlasting off-white."

Tricia stared in horror at the walls. "The paint is...their bones?"

Mrs. Tanser nodded. "It seemed a sacrilege to paint over the remains of those poor souls, so the room has been left exactly as it was when Pastor Martin sat down here in the middle of the room and... well... there's no delicate way to put this. He blew his brains out with a hunting rifle. Lord knows where he got it, a man of the clergy and all. Someone wiped down the ceiling and wall over there..." she pointed to a shadowy stain to their right.

"But all in all, the bones of those children are still right here, chalky and white, for anyone to see."

"Oh my dear, you're trembling; you're white as the walls. Come here, I'm so sorry. I'm an old woman and talk too much. I forget myself. And you, just a fifth grader and all. Let's have us a soda pop, hmmm?"

Mrs. Tanser pulled the wide-eyed girl from the room and bolted the lock once again.

"Don't need any of those summer breezes or restless ghosts getting in," she mumbled, and then shook her head. "Darn it all, there I go again."

* * * * *

The massive door opened with a long squeak. Mrs. Tanser peered through the foot-wide opening with a suspicious look on her face. Then her eyes lighted on the tousled hair of Tricia.

"You're probably here to see my nieces, aren't you?" she asked.

The girl shook her head. "No ma'am. I don't know them."

"Don't know them?" Mrs. Tanser looked confused. Then she slapped a palm to her forehead. "My oh, my, that's right. They came a-visiting awhile before you came a-visiting. And you've been too polite to correct an old woman before."

She opened the door wider and motioned Tricia inside. "Sometimes it's all a blur," she confided, and pushed the door shut.

"I remember now. I've been giving you the history of the house, and fattening you up on apples. Not the best choice for fattening, I'll give you, but it's what I have. No chocolate cakes up here on the hill!"

Mrs. Tanser motioned her into the kitchen.

"Where were we last time? I told you about the Whites and the Martins... There were others too. But then in the '50s, they turned the place into an orphanage."

Mrs. Tanser laughed. "I know, it sounds ridiculous. A house where children kept dying in horrible ways. A house where children's bones actually painted the walls white – and they turned it into an orphanage. But there you go. I wonder if they ever even saw the irony."

The rhythmic sound of a knife on stone filled the kitchen as Mrs. Tanser cut the girl an apple.

"Here we go," the older woman said, pushing a plate in front of the girl. She stared at the ceiling a moment and then grinned and nodded. "Forty-seven."

Mrs. Tanser scooped the core of the apple and a couple seeds from the counter and threw them in a waistcan. "Forty-seven children in all disappeared while this house was an orphanage. That's what I found out down there at the village hall. God knows why the town didn't have this place bulldozed, but, then again, who cares so much about orphans?"

The old woman shook her head in obvious disgust and then motioned for Tricia to follow her.

"Grab an apple," she said. "I want to show you something."

Mrs. Tanser led the way past the dining room and a dark hallway and the horrible room of bone paint, with its locked door. She stopped at another door, this one painted dark as a 2 a.m. shadow.

She pulled a ring of keys from the depths of her apron and

explained, "sometimes at night, I hear voices from in here. Terrible voices. Men howling. Children screaming. When I open the door, they're never there... but I keep it locked anyway."

She pushed the door open and stepped inside. Tricia followed, though hesitantly.

The room expanded to fill the eye with a vista of beautiful stonework and a floor of intricate mosaic. Like most of the house, the predominant color was no color. The room hurt the eye in its melding of cream and vanilla and starving, emaciated white. It also ascended three stories in the air and ran as deep as a football field.

"Over here," Mrs. Tanser called, and led Tricia to a corner. She reached down to the floor and pulled on a small cord that poked out from beneath the shards of tile. A hidden trap door opened upwards at her pull.

"Look," Mrs. Tanser pointed, and Tricia leaned in to stare down into the gap. The trap secreted a small cubbyhole, maybe 18 inches deep and a foot wide. Its bottom was hidden by dozens of small white pebble-like shards. They covered the bottom and stacked on top of each other like a pound of gravel.

"Hold out your hand," Mrs. Tanser said. As Tricia did, her arm visibly shook.

The older woman squeezed her outstretched palm and grinned. "It's OK. They can't get you here. There time was a long time ago. Now. You see these?" She turned the girl's hand palm side up and ran a finger across the top joint, on the other side of the fingernail.

"I'm not sure what they intended, but I believe that little stack of bones down there are the top joints of all those missing orphans' fingers."

Tricia ripped her hand away and gasped.

Mrs. Tanser shook her head. "They say down in town that those orphans disappeared, but it's no mystery where they went."

She let the trap fall down with a smack that echoed through the too-still room.

"Just look around you," she said and gestured at the intricately laid floor. "Those kids never left this room. Their bones are here, laid into the walls and the floor and the ceiling. Those kids built this room."

Tricia's eyes had now widened so large that the whites of her eyes were circled in red.

"Yep," the old woman sighed. "You're standing on them."

The girl screamed.

"Just bones," Mrs. Tanser said. "I wanted you to see, to understand. This house has a bad reputation, and rightly so. I'm sure those voices I hear coming from this room are from all those innocent orphans who had their fingers cropped off, and their bones ground down to shards of decorative tile."

"It's this house," she said and shook her head, pulling Tricia closer. The girl didn't fight her embrace. All she could think of was that she was standing on the chopped up bones of dead people.

"Everyone who's ever lived here has felt the need to add to the house," Mrs. Tanser said, and pulled the girl towards the back of the long room.

"The White House was large by the standards of the 1800s when Mr. White built it, but there have been many rooms added since. I showed you the draughty room last time you were here. And this room – which I think was probably a gymnasium for the orphans – was built over a long period. There are others. In the basement is a small closet that I believe was painted in the paste of a child… its colors are faded and dulled now, but it looks to be a mad swirl of mud and blood and bone if you stare closely. There's a shed on the back of the property that has window frames that are rounded and made of what looks to be rib bones. And the lock on that shed is a primitive thing, but it seems to be made of an arm or a leg bone that drops into place and holds the door fast."

"There's no way the realtor could have warned me," Mrs. Tanser said. "There's no way she could ever really have known – she wouldn't even stand inside this house. I wish she could have told me what I was in for. But the house… once you're here…"

They walked across the long bone mosaic room, and the chatter of Tricia's teeth began to reverberate through the silence.

"It's ok, child," Mrs. Tanser said. "I just want to show you one more room."

At the back of the long white room she stopped, and reached out to turn the latch on a door that only announced itself as thin seams set in the wall. It opened outward at her touch, and a cool breeze hit them as it did.

"I think that some of the rooms people added to the house were afraid to show their real colors," Mrs. Tanser said. "The people knew what they were doing, on some level, and they bleached the bones and carved the bones and crushed the bones into paste and mortar and paint."

"But when the house told me... when I realized what I would have to do, I made a pledge to myself to be true to the children who came here. The people who grew this house. They shouldn't be hidden in pieces, I said to myself, but celebrated. After all, every thing has its place. And every place, its thing. The things that build this house, have their place. They had life, and in death... they grow the White House in rooms of bone.

"And this house... must have its thing. These days... that's me."

Mrs. Tanser picked up a hammer and raised it above Tricia's head. She breathed deep as the girl squealed and tried desperately to run. Her screams rang out like bullets scraping metal. But Mrs. Tanser's other hand held the small girl fast. A trapped animal.

"You'll live here forever," she promised. "And I promise you'll hardly feel a thing. I can't believe the torture some of these kids must have gone through. I could never be so cruel."

Tricia screamed again. A horrible, larnyx-shredding sound. But she couldn't break free of the old woman's grip. Mrs. Tanser lived only for the house now, and Tricia had never felt such desperate strength before. The veins of the woman's hands stood out blue and serious above the small girl's reddening fingers. "I came to this town because I loved children. Genna and Jillie didn't want to stay here either," she whispered. "Look at them up there." She nodded at two tiny skulls shrieking in silence on the wall. "But what could I do? I adore children. The house...This house... it never relents..."

"Hold still," Mrs. Tanser said. "I want your face to stay this beautiful, always."

Tricia twisted and turned, staring at the bone-white eyesockets and jaws of the handful of splintered skulls that lined the half-constructed wall of the small room like fractured masks. Those perfect, unblemished bone faces screamed silently in chorus with her, as Mrs. Tanser turned to make her kill.

"It's going to take a long time to finish this room," the old woman lamented. "But I *will* finish my room. Everything has its place. And every place, its thing. This room is mine."

She brought the hammer down.

SWALLOWING THE PILL

Gerard coughed into his beer, sending a puff of froth over the edge. He turned his face away so the foam would drip from his chin to the floor instead of wetting his lap.

"Jeez man, you need some codeine. And an antibiotic. You sound terrible."

Gerard nodded mutely, willing the spasms to still in his tickling, wheezing throat. "Got some," he gasped finally. "Can't swallow the damn antibiotic pills though. They're effin' horse pills."

Andy laughed and shook his head. "Whaddya mean you can't swallow them?"

Gerard knew that behind the question was an accusation, the same disbelieving put-down that he'd heard from pharmacists all his life. *What are you, a baby or something? Be a man and take your medicine.*

"Believe me, I've tried, I just can't get them down."

"It's not a matter of can't, Ger," Andy clapped him on the shoulder. "It's a matter of won't. Your throat is big enough to accommodate the pill, but your mind says no. It's all in your head, my friend. If you really wanted to, you *could* swallow those pills."

Gerard coughed again, a prolonged hacking that left his chest prickling with deep, burning fire. He shook his head again, sniffed wetly and then shrugged.

"No, I'm serious here," Andy pushed, refusing to let the subject drop. "I don't believe your body is physically capable of floor vaulting from one end of this bar to the other – that's just not in your genes. But swallowing a pill..."

Gerard refused to argue anymore, and quenched the fire in his lungs with another draught of beer. Andy leaned closer, whispering so nobody else at the bar could hear.

"You can do whatever you want. Don't you realize that?"

Gerard squinted sidelong at his friend. "Whaddya talking about?"

"OK, take your boss, "the Harpy." You're always complaining that the bitch takes shit out on you. Well, give it back to her. And don't say you can't. OK, maybe you shouldn't knock her out physically because you'd get fired – and that would hurt you. But there are ways to get even. Ways that only you will know about. Piss in her coffee cup. Hack into her documents directory and delete all the records she worked on the day before. Shit like that. That'll teach the Harpy. You'll feel better."

Gerard shook his head. Andy was drunk again.

"Listen to me. Haven't you ever wondered what you're really capable of?"

Again Gerard shook his head. He was really wishing he'd stayed home tonight. In his bed.

"Man, you take everything lying down. You don't try. Push the envelope a little. I mean, shit, when you found out about Jenine and her boss, what did you do?"

Gerard slumped a little and mumbled something.

"What?"

"I said I forgave her."

"You forgave her. You didn't scream at her, wail on her or give her anything that she deserved."

"No. I couldn't hurt her, she's my wife. I loved her. I still do."

"Ah, and there's where you're wrong champ. You *could've* hurt her. She deserved some hurt for what she did to you. Hell, she might have even *appreciated* it. And you would have felt more like a man if you had."

Gerard looked away and Andy grabbed his shoulder.

"The very least you could've done is had a little of your own on the side. You've told me about that admin girl at work. What's her name? Trish? You said she comes on to you – so take her up on it."

"No. I can't."

Andy sighed, exasperated. "OK, I'll make you a deal: Think about this. Every time you say to yourself 'I can't do that' this week, I want you to force yourself to do it anyway."

"Forget it," Gerard whispered.

"No, c'mon. You worried about going to hell? You don't do

church, so if there is a hell, you're going there anyway."

Gerard sighed. "There's no hell, I know that."

"Well then. Time for you to break some boundaries, my man. C'mon, promise – every day this week you're going to do something that you say 'I can't' about. By this time next week, I guarantee you, that pill will be going down your throat without a second thought."

"Yeah right," Gerard laughed. "If I boff Trish I'll be able to swallow a pill all of a sudden? Get real."

"It's not about doing Trish or not doing Trish," Andy hissed. "It's about pushing yourself. It's about getting beyond all those little walls you've put up that don't do you or anyone else a bit of good. You can do whatever you want, man. For once quit staring at the ground and try to see what you're really capable of. I guarantee you, the world will be a much different place for you."

*   *   *   *   *

Gerard slept badly and dreamed worse. His nightmares were peopled with choking pills and stabbing knives and beautiful women who grabbed him by his silk tie and dragged him beneath a sea of black water.

Jenine was already in the shower when he staggered to the bathroom feeling worse than he had the day before. When was he going to shake this cold?

"How ya feeling honey?" came a silky voice from behind the curtain. Splashes of water slapped at the shower tile as she soaped her head and underarms.

"Worse," he croaked, and uncapped the horsepill bottle. Andy was right. He didn't try hard enough. He filled the bathroom cup with cold water and stared at the long daisy yellow pill in his hand. Then, closing his eyes, he tilted his head back and brought a hand up to his mouth. His other hand brought up the cup and with a gulp of cool liquid, he sent the pill to the back of his throat.

Where it lodged.

His eyes popped open and he shook his head in panic and the remaining water gurgled from between his lips into the sink. Leaning over the basin he coughed violently, freeing the pill to shoot from his throat to lie on the silver ring at the bottom of the sink. Tears wet the corners of his eyes as Jenine peered out from the curtain, black hair white with shampoo foam.

"OK?" she asked. He nodded quickly, not daring to talk. Replacing the cup in the holder by his toothbrush, he left the bathroom to her once again.

As Andy had so often reminded him, Gerard was a bit of a doormat. In college, with his boyish face and weight-bench augmented biceps, he'd never lacked for dates. But he'd also never been the one to call the relationships off. He was dumped and dumped on. Things hadn't really ever changed. Now at work he carried the yoke of blame for every department misstep, and at home his wife had, at least temporarily, dumped him over for another man. Gerard accepted it all and called himself lucky. Well, sometimes. It was easier to just take it and not cause a scene. Not that he didn't fume inside. He amused himself, placated himself, really, by imagining scenes where he took his petty revenges and emerged victorious from his complacency. But every fantasy held a bitter undercurrent of self-loathing. Because he could never act any of them out.

These thoughts dogged him all the way to work, and still nipped at his heels as he walked down the hallway, finding himself trailing Trish. Her miniskirted bottom bounced enticingly in front of him. He glanced around furtively, but there was no one else in the hallway.

You can't.

The voice was right, there was no way he could...nonetheless, Gerard reflexively brought his hand back.

You can't.

...and connected with a solid slap on that spongey rear.

She turned to him – blue eyes wide, jaw dropped, red glossed lips in a wide 'O' like the openmouthed Trish he'd imagined kneeling before him a thousand times before.

"Wha..."

"Hey Trish," he said simply and winked. "See you around."

She looked confused for a moment, then laughed. "OK."

* * * * *

That was the beginning.

It was a corner turned. Almost every hour afterwards, Gerard began testing himself in other ways. His imagination had never lacked for ideas.

Freed from his self-imposed shackles, Gerard explored his liberation like a convict emerging from a life-sentence. His feet were hot, sweating. They kept the office building too warm in his hallway. No windows to suck out the overflow of heat. With the toe of his right foot, he touched his left heel...

You can't...

and kicked off first the left shoe, then...

what are you doing? This is an office...

...his right.

Sitting back in his desk like a cheap parody of a pompous executive, he let his dogs out for a walk on the desk.

Instead of going outside in the cold to have a smoke...

You can't!

...he lit up in his office with the door closed until it looked like a London pea souper inside.

And then, high on the nicotine and codeine and just plain insanity of it, he slipped his slacks down to the floor, pulled out his penis, and lovingly enjoyed a vision of Trish, breasts pressed to his thighs, mouth pressed to his...

It felt good.

In his heart, he knew it was too good to be true. You couldn't just run rampant and expect to get away with it. The axe would fall. The Harpy would fire him somehow. Then Jenine would leave him, probably go back to sleeping with her boss.

His intercom crackled with Trish's voice, still a little uneven after their encounter in the hall, it seemed. "I'm sorry to be the bearer of bad news, but the Harpy wants you in her office, Gerard. Like NOW."

Gerard smiled.

*   *   *   *   *

Now, as he sat in front of Angela Harper's well-polished mahoghany desk, he thought again of Andy's taunts of the night before. The spill of shrill rhetoric spun past his ears like harmless cotton candy in the wind. It was Angela who had fucked up this time. It was her paperwork that was amiss. But as usual, she was playing pin the tail on Gerard with a tirade of self-righteous vinegar. Idly he stared at her coffeecup and grinned at Andy's suggestion. No...he could go one better. He could serve the bitch coffee AND cream. And she'd drink it all down and like it.

"*Yeah, right,*" his inner-self laughed. "*Like you could ever have the balls to do that. Peeling off your loafers and sneaking a smoke in the office is one thing, but this is the big enchilada. You can't. You CAN'T.*"

But what if he could? What stopped him, really? Maybe it was the codeine, but he warmed at the thought. Hell, he got hard at the thought.

A spat of coughing made him bring his own cup to his lips, all the while nodding and pretending to humbly accept Angela's abuse. The mug was empty. And from somewhere, he found himself saying:

"I'm sorry, Angela. I need a bathroom break. And some more coffee. Do you want me to get you some?"

Her thin lips stopped in mid-sentence, amazed that he would dare interrupt her, yet eager for more caffeine to power her vitriol.

"If you must," she said, holding out her mug haughtily. "But be quick about it. We need to straighten this out ASAP."

His hand was cold as he gripped himself in the stall, but the vision of Angela's lips sucking down what he intended to give her warmed him. He thought of his wife, taking the cock of another man down her throat (*how could she...?*) and then of Trish, kneeling right here in front of him, blouse undone to her navel...

The black liquid swirled into the mug, its heat dissolving Gerard's revenge like sugar. He topped it off with a splash of half and half and took the two cups back to Angela's office, groin lax and warmly sending out signals of satiation, heart meanwhile pounding with a mix of disgust, fear and excitement. What on earth was he doing?

But, oh God, it felt good watching her drink his little surprise down, licking her lips as if he tasted sweet as candy. And maybe he did. He certainly felt a rush that was sweeter than any candy in his heart. For once, Gerard Ambrose had the last laugh. Andy was right. Revenge, silent or not, brought a whole new view of the world. When the last of the coffee had disappeared between Angela's pale, frosty lips, Gerard could scarcely suppress a small, secret smile.

And then, high on the moment, he did something else unto-
ward.

You can't.

I can do anything I want.

You can't.

"You know Angela, if you'd filed the right paperwork for this
with the home office, we wouldn't be having this conversation,"
he said out loud, shocking himself nearly as much as her. "It's not
my problem. You figure it out."

And rising suddenly, he snatched his coffee cup in one hand and
turned his back on her. He did not have to suffer this. His exit was
marred by a spate of deep croupy coughs, but behind him, Angela
sat speechless, lips coated in the residue of her special coffee.

His mind was awash with conflicting emotions; self loathing
arm-in-arm with a rare appearance from self-love as he walked
through the garage entryway into his kitchen. The TV was blaring in the background and Jenine came rushing in from the living
room, her kinked black hair frizzed up as if she'd been sleeping
on it.

"Hon, would you go back out and pick up some dinner," she
begged, planting a dry, chaste kiss on his lips. "I didn't have
time..."

Automatically, Gerard did an about face, then broke into
another fit of coughing that left him bent over, wheezing for air.

You can't...

"No," he said quietly. Without another word he went up the
stairs to change, absently noting that the bedsheets were a mess,
something Jenine never put up with. So.

He stripped naked, walked to the bathroom and swallowed
half the bottle of codeine cough syrup. As the hot trickle warmed
his throat and spread its flame to his belly, he climbed into those
sheets, still musty with the scent of his wife's sex. She did not join
him.

This time, however, he did not cry himself to sleep.

When he awoke, Jenine's perfume still hung in the air of the
bedroom, but the house was silent. She'd left for work already,
without a word. She knew that he knew. And what could she possibly say?

He coughed himself awake and went through his morning

routine. Lather, rinse, gargle, comb. The wheels were now turning faster than ever before. And yet he was so calm. Almost emotionless. The antibiotic bottle mocked him from the sink. Soon.

At work, Trish paged him to help her with a software glitch, and as he leaned over her shoulder, smelling the flowery explosion of her hair, he reached out a...

You ca...

...hand and cupped her right breast. It was full, deliciously heavy in his hand. She looked up at him—surprised—but but didn't pull away.

"I thought..." She didn't finish her sentence.

"Cook me some dinner tonight. I want to see how you live," he said, staring directly into her eyes.

Her gaze dimmed a moment, then her eyes locked with his. She looked afraid. Then nodded.

✦   ✦   ✦   ✦

Trish's apartment was purple. Lavender carpet, violet drapes. Her bedroom walls were pink with a bed topped by royal purple sheets and comforter. Her body felt as silky as the sheets, and Gerard entered her without ...

You c...

...a condom. Her mouth sucked his own inside of her, and for a moment, he remembered the flash of searing ecstasy he'd once felt with his wife as she took him within her. When she was his and only his...

He bit wildly at her neck and bosom and she raked her hands down his back, first in passion, then with frantic insistence.

Gerard swam back from the brink of ... something ... to see her widened eyes and hear her cries of "No, no, no!"

He pushed himself off of her, red welts already swelling on her skin, tears streaming from her eyes.

He didn't say anything, just pulled his pants and shirt on. In a second he was out the door, coat in hand. Trish wasn't the woman he felt this way about. His problems were at home.

* * * * *

The house was dark when he got in, but her car was in the garage. He hardly even thought now about what he ...

You...

...was going to do.

The rope slipped around her sleeping wrists and ankles with ease. She didn't even stir until he was lifting her up from the bed.

"Where?" she asked sleepily.

"I could say the same," he said.

He laid her in the bathtub. Stopper down.

"I can't take any more," he said, as if that explained it all. Her eyes widened as she tested the tightness of her bindings and he leaned over her to tie the gag. Her head shook wildly and he sighed, loudly.

"Once I could forgive, but twice..." She started arching her back, trying to flop herself out of the tub, and with hardly a ...

You...

...thought, he brought his hand down on her face. With five sharp raps on the tile, she was still.

Then he went to the garage.

The chlorine barrels for the pool were heavy, but he had managed to get them from the store to the trunk before. And so he managed to cart them through the kitchen, up the stairs and into the bathroom.

Slipping a razor from his Bic, he sliced through the thin cotton of her night shirt, and then her panties, leaving her naked and unconscious on the bottom of the tub. He looked at her then, slack lips parted, hair curled in ringlets up the sides of the tub, where soap and a trickle of blood had pasted it. Soft, full breasts ripe for kissing and a belly that even now brought a throb to his pants.

Enough. You can do anything. You've proved it already. You've punished her. You can't....

Methodically, he emptied the jugs of chlorine into the tub, watching with a scientific indifference as the yellow fluid crept up between her thighs, soaked her, and then covered the closely-cropped tuft of secret hair below her belly.

How long would it take for her skin to burn away? he wondered.

She stirred then, and her eyes opened. They looked foggy, confused. And then, in pain.

"I'm not buying dinner tonight," he said coughing. The fumes were stifling now, and Gerard started coughing again. Grabbing his medicine, he left her alone in the bath, closed the door and went down the stairs to the kitchen. His eyes were watering and he poured a tall glass of milk from the fridge. There was a dull pounding sound echoing from upstairs, but he couldn't think about that, he couldn't seem to stop coughing; his chest was an agony of phlegmy irritation. Uncapping the bottle of antibiotics, Gerard popped one in his mouth and took a gulp of milk.

Y...

The pill went down easy.

PUMPKIN HEAD

Jack's hands trembled as he traced a small circle on the slick skin of the pumpkin, using a magic marker and the bottle-cap he'd lifted from his mom's medicine cabinet. It looked to be about the right size.

A gibbous moon shone in garish relief off the night-polished hides of hundreds of orange globes, but Jack's chosen pumpkin was special. He'd picked it for its size as well as its seclusion. Somehow, this particular vine had crept over the irrigation ditch and nurtured its offspring well away from the others under the shade of a gnarled elm.

The tiny circle drawn, Jack opened his pocketknife and with quick, short thrusts turned his drawing into a hole. His heart began pumping with growing volume as he completed the first stage of his violation.

"You've got to try this!" Tom had told him in a whisper the previous week after school. Exhaling a cloud of Marlboro smoke with practiced disdain for anyone who might be staring his way, Tom had laughed. "It's so twisted, it's great. You just have to make sure the hole's not too big, or it won't work."

At first, he'd figured Tom had to be making it up. *Nobody would try that!* Totally gross. But every time he thought about it, he got a funny feeling inside; the idea attracted him. And so tonight, under the chill wind of an October moon, Jack stood holding a pumpkin coring. *This was stupid*, he thought for the hundredth time. *This is warped.*

But after taking a furtive glance around the pumpkin patch behind him, silently amazed at the endless rows of orange bas-ketball shapes stretching to the black horizon, Jack unbuckled his belt and dropped his jeans to the ground. A cold knot twisted his stomach at the realization that he was going through with this perversion, and a countering hot stab of anticipation drove through his heart and groin. With a shiver and a shrug, he shoved his underpants past his knees and, goosebumps popping out across his bare lower body, knelt next to the pumpkin.

Gripping the rough, wrinkled skin of the dead vine atop the gourd, Jack guided his straining penis into the newly sawn receptacle. He gasped aloud at its touch. He was afraid at first - would the hole be large enough to receive him? Would he be trapped inside? Would he catch some weird pumpkin disease - orange genital warts?

But none of these concerns stopped him from pressing through the gently resisting cavity. It was cold, sticky. He imagined his favorite pin-up girl lying here in the leaves and brush before him. *She'd be warmer*, he thought, but sticky too. *Would she feel like this?* He stifled a moan as he pressed into a new area of slimy seeds and pumpkin hair. Jack moved close to embrace all of the warty hide of the pumpkin as its jellied hairs tickled and caressed his member inside. It felt as if it was moving with him, pulling at him to stay as he arched away. He'd cut the hole just right. It was tight enough to grip him like a woman. Or, as good as he thought a woman might. *A woman filled with cold slime and seeds*, he laughed, the thought driving him to cleave hard to the lined sides of the gourd. He uttered one more involuntary gasp of pleasure as the tremors of release rocked him and left. And then clammy fear at the extant of his depravity gripped him. What had he done here?

Rolling away from his vegetable mate, he yanked his pants up, not even bothering to wipe off the commingled strands of orange and white mucus. It gelled in the hair on his groin and belly, a sticky accusation of his strange and darkly pleasurable fornication. He tucked two pumpkins under his arms as he stole away from the quiet field on the edge of town.

"Where'd you get those?" he mother yelled as he went dashing through the kitchen with his stolen treasures. "Don't take them upstairs, they'll rot! Jack!"

Depositing the pumpkins safely in his room, he returned to the kitchen to assuage his mother. The trick with her was to get things settled before she got talking about it. Then she wouldn't bother forcing him to change.

"I'm gonna carve them up there," he announced, staving off her objections. "Halloween's in a couple days, and they won't rot before then. If I leave them outside kids'll kick 'em through the street."

She looked uncertain, and he pressed his advantage. "I'll clean up everything, don't worry."

* * * * *

That night, after turning out the light, Jack ran his hands lightly over the smooth, bumpy skins of his pumpkins. Their texture drove a shiver through his bod. His groin jumped. Whitely naked and bent beneath the moonlight glinting through his bedroom window, Jack kissed his pumpkins good night, and then dove guiltily into bed. His saliva glittered in beads on the dark orange skins.

* * * * *

Jack had thought he'd share his experience with Tom if he went through with it - after all, it had been Tom who'd clued him in, right? But when he got to school the next day and saw his friend's cynical sneer as he joked about getting a piece of Mary Scott, Jack realized that he and his pumpkin queen were a private item.

That night, with the bedroom door locked, he once again traced the bottlecap on a pumpkin and punched through its pale pulpy hymen. His hips moved faster, sliding the pumpkin and himself across the floor as he fought to stay with his new lover. But as he stifled a grunt of orgasmic reaction, it was his first pumpkin that he found himself thinking of.

The next night he found himself fidgeting at the dinner table. Meatloaf and carrots with cauliflower covered his plate. The orange and white of his vegetables lay in front of him, reminding him of his newfound carnal pleasures. And it excited him. He was dying to get away from the table to lock himself away for precious moments with his pumpkin. But when he finally got there, when he'd carved a new hole and sluttishly spent himself, once again he found himself craving the attentions of his first, the monstrous pumpkin queen who's insides had seemed to suck him to ecstasy that first time. Tucking his gluey dick back in his pants, Jack quickly scooped and finished carving his first pumpkin. He had to have some evidence for his rush to get to his room.

"Oh, that's very, um, niiice, Jack" his mom said as he showed off his newly carved pumpkin. She looked puzzled. "I thought it was supposed to be scary though, hon."

"So, this one's a happy pumpkin," Jack shrugged and went back upstairs to clean up.

✳   ✳   ✳   ✳   ✳

He got two more rides – one after school and one after dinner – out of the next pumpkin before carving it up into a face which his mother, in utter puzzlement, pronounced beautiful. In years past, Jack's pumpkins had always held a certain demonic terrorism in their fangs and slanted eyes. But these - she stared at the two demure smiles on the orange globes on the kitchen table - these were ... coquettes.

✳   ✳   ✳   ✳   ✳

"I'm going trick or treating for awhile," Jack announced, letting the door slam behind him before there could be protest. She thought he was too old to go, but why should the little runts get all the free candy? He'd borrowed Tom's football jersey and helmet and set off. It was a windy Halloween, and an earlier rain had set a bone-slathering chill in the air. Leaves rustled and dropped wetly all around him as he worked his way block by block to the end of town. The moon was small and piercingly white by the time he admitted where he'd been edging his way to. At last he called off the charade. Breaking into a run, Jack sprinted with a shopping bag full of candy the remaining four blocks to the pumpkin field. He'd thought about her – his first, his pumpkin queen – all through school. The gourds he'd brought home simply hadn't fulfilled him like her. He prayed she was still there. He prayed she hadn't rotted from the hole he'd gored into her side.

The pumpkin field was a dismal sight on Halloween night. Only the rejects were left here now: the misshapen, rotted, too-small pumpkins littered the field, seemingly in large numbers; but the deep dark depressions where their brethren had but recently rested betrayed the extent of their abandonment. Jack loped through the field, heading toward the back ditch, anxious to reach the shelter of that crooked elm.

But she wasn't there. At first he thought he had the wrong tree, but then he saw the telltale deep depression she'd left, and his own rutted kneeprints beside it. *Who would have taken a pumpkin with a hole right in the middle of her best side?* he wondered, and sank to the ground. *How, HOW, had he become such a perve that he was lusting after a pumpkin? But, she'd been right here, so cool, so ... good!*

"Looking for someone?"

The voice at his back startled him to his feet.

"No no," he stammered, as he stared at the girl before him. She was naked, entwined in a vine that stretched from her belly to the ground beside him. She stepped closer, and his breath caught. She was orange. The deep, mottled orange of ripe pumpkin. She exuded a musky vegetable odor as she stepped closer and ran a warted finger up his face to poke into his open mouth.

"There was a pumpkin here," he said, pulling away and pointing to the hollow on the ground. The hollow near where her vine was embedded in earth.

"Yes," she answered, her voice a husky rustle of summer and seed. She touched him again, and he saw then that her skin, though smooth, was marred occasionally by dark warts and dimples. Wet-looking translucent strands of hair hung from her head and her crotch. He guessed that hair would be cool and sticky. As she wrapped her arms around him in askance, he found that he'd guessed correctly

"You were looking for my mother," she whispered like the wind in his ear. Her tongue, cool and wet, traced designs on his neck before she said, "That means you are the man who raped her. You are my father."

At that, she dropped to his waist and began tugging at his belt. "I will be the woman my mother could never have been for you," she promised, and slowly, he began to aid her in releasing his clothes. Common sense told him this was not what it seemed; pumpkins did not have human, albeit orange and warty, children. Girls did not give blowjobs to strange boys in fields. But here she was, and her cool touch was driving him to fever. He let her crawl across his skin. Her slimy kisses stuck to his skin like fruit pulp. His cock was so erect it was painful. He'd never been so aroused. Her breasts were hard, tipped by dark brown warts. And her hair was entangling itself on his body, ripping loose from her in sticky heaps. He felt it on his crotch from the pressure of her own, it was hidden in the crease of his neck like chilled sauerkraut.

And then she pulled back. Stretching out across the dirt where just days before he'd had her mother, she showed him the oval valley between her smooth, lightly creased legs. "You can have this," she promised. "I'll be better than my mother. But first, you'll have to cut my cord. She held the browning vine up from her belly, and with squeamish understanding, he dug through his discarded clothes for his pocketknife. Flipping open the blade, he held it as close as he could to her belly, and began sawing. She stiffened as he did, but said nothing. A clear, sticky fluid flowed across his knife and onto his hands, and it was over.

"Now," she said, her voice a rasp of longing. "Seed me, fertilize me, water me." In her tone, those words sounded like the dirtiest night talk Jack had ever heard. Without pausing to close his knife, he tossed it away and pressed his legs to hers.

This was like the first time, he thought as he bucked on top of the cool pumpkin girl. Her eyes glittered blackly in the moonlight beneath him as he kissed her hard lips, ran his tongue along the pulp ridge of her teeth. She sucked his heat into her, her natural frigidity only driving him to a hot wash of orgasm.

"Yes," she wheezed as he came at last, panting and flopping atop her like an epileptic. And then, as Jack looked to see if his lover's eyes were as satisfied as his own, he saw that her hunger had only just begun. "We will fertilize hundreds of seeds together, my love" she promised, encircling him in a grip of orange rind as solid as wood. He struggled, kicked, screamed. But there was no escaping the grasp of the pumpkin queen as in a flash, her arms and legs sealed around him and they began to roll as one downhill.

And who paid attention to muffled screams in the depth of night on Halloween?

They found his clothes eventually, underneath an old gnarled elm behind an empty pumpkin field. They were lying on bare earth; nearby a knife was stabbed crookedly in the dirt. As the farmer led police to the spot to search for further clues of the missing boy, he spied a huge orange pumpkin peeking through the weeds at the bottom of the hill. He shook his head at having missed such a prize pumpkin the week before.

It would have brought a good price.

Inside that "prize" gourd, a white-slimed shape contorted at the sound of voices. Kneading hands of pumpkin hair kept him in near-constant orgasm, and handful by handful, deposited orange-slick, newly formed white seeds into pockets on his flesh.

"We will fertilize hundreds of seeds together," she whispered, in words only he could hear.

In addition to his short fiction collection Most Curious, **Bill Breedlove's** *work has appeared in publications such as the* Chicago Tribune, RedEye, InSider, The Fortune News, Restaurants & Institutions, Encyclopedia of Actuarial Science, Bluefood.cc *and* Playboy Online. *His stories can also be found in the books* Tales of Forbidden Passion, Strange Creatures, Tails from the Pet Shop, Book of Dead Things, Cthulhu and the Coeds *and* Blood and Donuts.

In 2002, Bill's horror film screenplay Last of the True Believers *won a competition sponsored by* DAILY VARIETY *where the prize was a trip to the Cannes Film Festival to meet with Hollywood producers and executives.*

Bill lives in Chicago with his dog, Maestro. His website is www.curiousstories.com.

THE LOST COLLECTION

Charles Manson crept silently toward his unsuspecting victim, a menacing and entirely out-of-proportion sized butcher knife clutched in one gripping hand. His face wore a perpetual leer of evil and corruption – eyes slitted, mouth upturned into some unholy expression between a grimace and a sneer. As he moved closer, raising the knife, the young woman with the long blonde hair sat seemingly oblivious, scanning the rapidly darkening horizon with a vacant stare from her crystal blue eyes.

Just as he was about to pounce, another figure arrived on the scene: a grizzled, battle-scarred veteran wearing torn army fatigues and casually clutching an M-16. Manson straightened at the sight of this interloper. "You!" he hissed.

The other figure raised the M-16 until the barrel was even with Charlie's face. "Call me...Joe, scumbag," he said, and prepared to fire.

"Elliott! Elliott, where are you?" a woman's voice called crossly from the house. "You know I want you inside before dark."

Both Charlie and the solider dropped to the ground next to Barbie as Elliott grudgingly let them go and stood up to answer his mother's call. "Come on, Mom! I was only in the backyard!"

"Well," the voice from the house continued, "you know I don't like it when you're out there all alone in the dark. Come in and I'll make you some warm milk and graham crackers before bed."

"Awwww, Mom!" Elliott began, but it was no use, she had already left the window and gone to another part of the house. The debate was over, case closed.

Elliott looked down at his dolls. Joe and Barbie were filthy, having weathered many backyard adventures with Elliott. The Manson doll, however, was spotless. Elliott didn't play with him very much. And with good reason – he had gone through the dickens to get that doll.

So instead, Charlie, Jeffrey, Richard, John, Ted and rest of the crew sat mostly alone in Elliott's secret compartment in his toy trunk. If his mother ever found out he had managed to snag so many of the Bloodthirsty Murderers Collection, she would definitely freak out. Even worse, she might take the dolls away.

And THAT was something Elliott didn't want to happen. So, he gathered up his toys, careful to brush off some offending grass clippings from Charlie's wildly long and unkempt hair, and went inside.

✸   ✸   ✸   ✸

Elliott's father had been in the Army, so Elliott had moved a great deal in his twelve years. Elliott didn't mind moving so much, but Mom didn't like it, or so they said, and that was the reason why Dad and Mom didn't live together anymore.

But Elliott remembered well how it was to be the new kid, and so he empathized, when on Monday the teacher made a small boy stand up and face the class and said, "Everyone, this is Marty Clemmens, his family just moved here from…" she trailed off and looked at the boy quizzically.

"Two Forks, South Dakota," he prompted, looking shyly at the ground.

"South Dakota," Mrs. Peterson said brightly. "Now I am sure you will all go out of your way to make Marty here feel welcome." She let go of the boy's thin shoulders and put her hands on her hips. "Now who can tell me what the capital of South Dakota is?"

Elliott tuned out the teacher and watched the new boy slowly take his seat. There was something helpless seeming about the kid, as if he was more fragile than an average boy. Maybe he was a hemophiliac, Elliott's cousin Robbie was one of those, and he couldn't play sports, or even run with other kids. The slightest touch to his skin and a nasty bruise would immediately swell up on Robbie. Once, they had been standing in line together for Thanksgiving pie, and some dim reptile part of Elliott's brain had seized control for one second, and he had viciously poked poor Robbie in the upper arm, just to see what would happen. Robbie let out a yelp and the area around the poke had quickly turned a highly incriminating shade of crimson.

Elliott had been mortified. He had expected something, but nothing like the dramatic reaction which was taking place. As Elliott's and Robbie's parents came rushing over to see what all the commotion was about, Robbie began to cry, and as he did so, he fixed Elliott with such a look of pain and sadness that Elliott had begun to cry as well. The hastily mouthed apologies and barely insinuated recriminations were far less memorable to Elliott than that haunted look in Robbie's eyes.

"TOPEKA, KANSAS" the teacher's voice boomed off the chalkboard and walls decorated with cartoon animals and ambulatory numerals. It took Elliott a moment to realize that Mrs. Peterson was directing her thundering to him. He blinked, and she said, "If it's not TOO much trouble, Mister Warwick, please answer the question."

There were titters of laughter sprinkled throughout the classroom, but Elliott's attention was completely absorbed by the new boy, Marty Clemmens, who now turned slowly in his desk to meet Elliott's gaze.

Marty Clemmens had wide, watery blue eyes, which stared confidently back into Elliott's brown ones. As they looked at each other, Elliott felt something pass between; some type of bond was forged between the two boys. Marty's eyebrows raised a bit, reflecting that he too noticed some type of transference. Then, the moment had passed, and Marty turned back around in his chair and Elliott was left to confront the angry Mrs. Peterson and the rest of the giggling class.

Curiously, at lunch and afternoon recess, Marty was nowhere to be found. Elliott looked all over the playground for him, but there was no sign of the new boy. When the 3:15 bell rang, Elliott almost lost him again, but spotted him ambling alone down the back path, a frayed-looking purple backpack carelessly draped over one thin shoulder.

He ran to catch up, and only when he pulled alongside Marty did he stop to catch his breath. "Hey," he said, panting.

Marty turned and looked at him briefly. "Hey," he answered noncommittally.

They fell into step together, walking through the field behind the school. "New here, huh?" said Elliott when they had walked in silence for a few minutes.

"Yep."

"Do you like it here, I mean better than..." Where had he said his family moved from? Kansas? "Topeka?" Elliott asked

Marty turned and looked at him, "No, not Topeka. Two Forks. Two Forks, South Dakota."

"Oh yeah, right." Elliott could see that this wasn't going too well. "How long did you live there?"

Marty shrugged. "I dunno. Not long, I guess." He looked at Elliott again, longer this time. "We move around a lot."

"Dad in the army or something?" Elliot asked.

"Something." Marty said, without feeling the need to elaborate further.

"WELL..." Elliott tried again. "I know how it is to be the new kid a lot. My dad – when he used to live with me and my mom – was in the army, and we moved around a whole bunch." Marty was looking at him but saying nothing. "So, I, well, I know kinda how it is to be the new kid."

"Oh."

"SO ANYWAY," Elliott barreled onward, "I thought maybe you might want to come over to my house, and we could play guns or something."

Marty stopped walking, and Elliott stopped with him. "I don't really like to play guns," he said quietly.

"Oh," Elliott was nonplused.

"Do you like dolls?" Marty asked him. "I mean, like real cool dolls?"

"You mean, like the Bloodthirsty Murderers Collection?" Elliott replied.

"Exactly!" Marty said, "I LOVE the Bloodthirsty Murderers

Collection!"

Elliott could scarcely believe his luck. What a bonus! "I have lots of the Bloodthirsty Murderers," he said.

"Really?" asked Marty, showing real, unfeigned interest for the first time. "Like who?"

"Well, I have Manson, and Speck and Bundy and Gacy and Dahmer."

"Doesn't everybody?" Marty was shaking his head. "Which Manson?"

"The sixties, hippie, pre-swastika one, of course," Elliott answered. The toy company which manufactured the Bloodthirsty Murderers Collection, Imperial Toymakers, supposedly made more than one version of the Manson doll, its most popular product. But, the other Manson was rumored to be extremely rare. "You can't get the other one."

"Oh really?" Marty replied, somewhat haughtily, and unslung the pack from his bony shoulder. He unzipped it and began rummaging through. "Take a look at this."

He handed something wrapped in a towel to Elliott. Unwrapping it carefully, Elliott could not believe his eyes. It was a miniature likeness of Charles Manson, except in lieu of the tangled mass of hair, this one had a shaved head and was dressed in prison blues. An angry swastika glowered redly from the doll's forehead. The same malevolent stare was evident that adorned the face of Elliott's Charlie doll. The workmanship was really something to be commended.

"WOW!" Elliott said. "This is really neat!"

"So, what others do you have?" Marty asked, again, somewhat patronizingly.

"Well," Elliott began, still mesmerized by the doll in his hands. "I have Son of Sam."

"Yeah, so?"

"Oh, wait," Elliott had a burst of pride. "I have Albert DeSalvo." The Boston Strangler was one of the rarer members of the Bloodthirsty Murderers Collection, and he figured that should impress Marty.

"Ho hum," he said.

"Well, WHO else do you have?" Elliott asked, exasperated.

"Me? I have them ALL." Marty replied. And for emphasis he

added, "All of them, even the Lost Collection."

Silence followed this proclamation. Elliott was thunder-struck. Nobody, but nobody could have the entire collection – there were just too many rare dolls. Plus, it was not easy to track down stores carrying the Bloodthirsty Murderers Collection.

As it might be imagined, Imperial Toymakers faced a tremendous challenge when they decided to begin marketing the Bloodthirsty Murderers Collection. Not only was the public outraged, but multiple lawsuits by everyone from victims' families to the convicted themselves (at least those who were still alive) made it extremely difficult to get crucial shelf space at most major retailers. Of course, none of the big chains would touch the Collection, and in some small towns in the South, it was actually a felony to distribute or even possess any of the dolls.

Most parents forbade their children to even talk about the figurines, and it was next to impossible to get any advertising space on televisions or papers. However, cryptically-worded ads in the back of selected comic books and fanzines alerted the faithful on where portions of the Collection could be obtained.

Predictably, sales skyrocketed. The more strident the public outcry against the dolls, the keener the interest. At conventions, Bloodthirsty Murderers commanded top dollar, and eager children queued up in lines snaking across hotel ballrooms all across the country for a chance to plunk down hard-earned allowance money to take home a likeness of a particular favorite killer.

In the lip-service press releases which Imperial Toymakers sent out, their ostensible reason for marketing the Collection was "education." "If children learn from the mistakes of others, then the atrocities perpetrated by these individuals – atrocities which Imperial Toymakers, Limited and its subsidiaries, shareholders and Board of Directors absolutely do not condone – will serve as excellent reference material for inquiring young minds to avoid the horrors which could plague them."

Therefore, as part of the "educational component" in each doll's package was included trading cards with a full color (computer digitally colorized in the case of old photos) face portrait of the killer on the front, along with a helpful "stat sheet" on the back. Even more useful to the young scholar was the comic-like booklet "history of _____" which recounted – in glaring primary colors and lurid detail – each and every blood-splattered moment of a particular murderer's career.

Additionally, each doll came with an authentic set of accessories and outfits, whether it be a large plastic meat freezer, a tiny wrapped case of various knife blades, or an ingeniously realized clown costume complete with minuscule greasepaint applicators. All in the interest of – as Imperial Toymakers promotional materials trumpeted – "scrupulous historical detail."

Naturally, the airtight veil of secrecy surrounding Imperial Toymakers, their mobile factories and corporate headquarters – the address listed on the boxes was in reality a brothel in New Jersey – caused endless speculation among the faithful, who waited eagerly for some firsthand information about what and when new product was being added to the line.

Rumors grew up and dissipated like wildfire – new figurines, Imperial going out of business, a Congressional act to outlaw any more toys, etc. etc. However, the most pervasive rumor surrounding the Bloodthirsty Murderers line was of the fabled "Lost Collection." What exactly comprised this Lost Collection was anybody's guess, but the most popular story had it that the Lost Collection was made up of all of the dolls which were so hideous, so vile and so nasty that even the folks at Imperial Toymakers had been unable to run a full production line. So, after destroying the molds, only a few of these precious figures remained, and no one knew if they in fact existed, and if so, where they could be had.

Now, here was this new kid in town, not only sneering at Elliott's hard-won group of murderer dolls, but boasting of having each and every figurine produced by Imperial Toymakers, including the Lost Collection.

It was all a bit much.

"Oh yeah?" Elliott said, "Prove it."

Marty smiled thinly at him for a moment, and then produced another carefully-wrapped object from the depths of his backpack. As he ceremoniously removed it, Elliott had time to wonder if the new kid was completely crazy. At Shady Grove Elementary School – and virtually every institute of education, public or private – possessing a Bloodthirsty Murderer doll on school property was a offense warranting immediate expulsion. Even worse, confiscation of the toy in question was also a given.

"Here," Marty said, casually handing the object to Elliott.

Elliott unwrapped the heavy fabric and gazed disbelieving at the doll in his hands. It was of an older gentleman, wearing a tweed suit. His neatly cut white hair and impeccably trimmed mustache were clues, but the penetrating stare of the pale blue eyes gave it away. But it was impossible – this was a doll of Albert Fish, a notorious kidnapper/murderer/cannibal who had butchered and eaten many hapless children in the 1930s.

Albert Fish was number one on the list of the mythical "Lost Collection."

Elliott looked up at Marty. "No way!" he breathed.

Marty just smiled, as if he was used to precisely this type of reverent reaction. "It's true, all right, you can even check the back of his neck."

In order to avoid the obvious problems of unauthorized duplication and copyright infringement, all official members of Imperial Toymakers Bloodthirsty Murderers Collection had a small mark – similar to a tattoo – on the back of their necks, just below the hairline. This complicated and extremely difficult to reproduce mark was Imperial's "Guarantee of Authenticity." Sure enough, right there on the back of the neck was the mark. It was genuine.

Elliott felt like his whole being must be shaking. The sinister figure in his hands must be worth hundreds, maybe thousands of dollars, and yet, Marty didn't seem too concerned about letting him hold it. "What other ones do you have?" he asked breathlessly.

Marty carefully extracted the doll from Elliott's sweaty grasp. He smiled again, "Too many to list... too many."

"Oh," Elliott said.

Suddenly, Marty seemed to brighten. "Wanna come see 'em?" he asked.

"What?" Elliot said, startled. "Where?"

"My house isn't too far from here," Marty said.

"I don't know," Elliott offered. "I probably should be getting home."

"Oh, OK," Marty said, voice inflectionless. "I thought maybe you were a serious collector. I thought maybe you wanted to see the Lost ones."

"There's more?" Elliot asked, astonished.

Marty beamed at him. "Lots more."

Elliott stopped walking along the path a moment to think. Here was a golden opportunity to see an entire collection of Bloodthirsty Murders... maybe one of the only collections in the world. And this new kid was offering to show it to him for free – just because he had been nice and tried to befriend him. Elliott thought happily that his mother was indeed right, good deeds do get rewarded.

"Sure, but I can't stay long."

"That's OK," Marty said, "it won't take too long."

Onward they walked, and Elliott lost track of time and distance as he asked Marty question after question about both the Bloodthirsty Murderers Collection and savage killers in general. The kid was like a walking encyclopedia, filling in gaps in Elliott's knowledge of some of the more infamous exploits of the last hundred years or so.

Finally, they came to a house well away from the road, in fact a house Elliott had only seen two or three times in his lifetime and which he had heard was abandoned. It sure looked to be in disrepair. "This is your house?" he asked confusedly.

"Well, we like a lot of land and privacy, and we got it for really cheap my dad said." Marty said, and proceeded to the side door. "It's still kind of messy because we haven't really unpacked yet, but that doesn't matter, because all the dolls are in the basement."

"The basement?" Elliott asked. "Why?"

"It's my mom, you know?" Marty offered a shrug. "She says she gets the creeps from all the dolls being in my room, so I have to put them somewhere where she doesn't have to look at them."

Marty reached into his shirt and produced a key attached to a piece of rawhide tied around his neck. He inserted it into the lock and grinned at Elliott. "Get ready for this."

Descending the stairs, Elliott was half expecting the basement to be a cobwebby, dusty place with old musty smelling boxes of toys stacked haphazardly in the gloom. He was not prepared for what he saw.

It was a shrine.

Immaculately presented on all four walls were hundreds of

dolls. Each wall had a special shelving unit attached to it, which made every doll have its own separate compartment to stand upright in. From floor to ceiling, row upon row of murderous insanity in tiny plastic form. Killers from across the ages graced the room, all garbed in authentic period dress, down to the smallest detail. Here was Lizzie Borden, in a high-necked black Victorian dress, stained axe in her hand. There was Jack the Ripper, scalpel at the ready, brownish kidney clutched in between two long fingers.

"Wow," was all Elliot could say.

"Impressive, aren't they?" Marty agreed.

"Amazing." Elliot whispered. It seemed appropriate not to speak loudly.

He glanced around the room, at this Who's Who of murder and mayhem. In the dark, the dolls' eyes seemed to glitter, thousands of little eyes looking back at him from faces possessed by unspeakable madness. Elliott felt gooseflesh break out all along his arms, and turned to look for Marty.

He was no longer standing next to Elliott, but was inserting a key into another door in the side of the basement. "Well, thanks, but I think I have to get going now," Elliott said, in a rather pathetic squeak.

Marty turned from the door and looked at him quizzically. "I thought you wanted to see the Lost Collection?" he asked.

"I have, and now I'm ready to go home," Elliott said, aware that his voice had taken on the petulant, whining tones of a spoiled child.

Marty knit his brows in honest puzzlement. "What do you mean?" He looked around the basement. "Those are nothing... in here" he said, motioning to the other room, "here is what you came to see."

Elliott could only feebly shake his head as Marty crossed over to him and gently took his hand, propelling him through the doorway. "This is the Lost Collection."

Elliott looked around the room. If anything, this room was even more magnificent that the other. At least ten times as many dolls lined the walls in here, thousands upon thousands of dolls. But what made them even more astonishing was their condition.

Almost every doll was covered in blood, some had one or

more limbs missing, others were in several pieces. Some, which were so hacked up as to be virtually unrecognizable, were held in place by chicken wire and model airplane glue.

Elliott turned confusedly to Marty, "Who are they? Are they..." He trailed off.

Marty shook his head. "Yes. They're the victims. The Lost."

Looking closer now, Elliot was able to see just how much work had been put into setting up this collection. Each section was divided, so that the killer was grouped among his victims. For example, a skinny pock-marked doll surrounded by eight woman dolls in crisp white nurse uniforms was obviously Richard Speck. Similarly, a portly John Wayne Gacy doll lolled among a gaggle of broken boy figurines.

Elliott saw a replica of his own Charles Manson doll, along with Tex Watson and Squeaky Fromme, and among them their victims. He picked up the exquisitely beautiful doll of the pregnant actress, and sure enough, a tiny plastic detachable fetus was enclosed in the belly, evidence of Imperial Toymakers unflinching commitment to historical authenticity.

Elliott looked around at the display, eyes bugging in their sockets. Something was wrong with one of the groups, and it took him a minute to deduce what it was. There was one set which quite obviously was missing figures. It was on the first shelf, lower to the floor, in a place of apparently not much significance, and Elliott had to stoop to look at it.

Curiously, he didn't immediately recognize any of the figurines. They were mostly children, with only two adult victims, a man and a woman. Elliott picked up the Bloodthirsty Murderer figurine and looked it over closely. Something was odd about this one, and he realized with a start that it was much smaller than the others, like it was a midget... or a child.

Marty's voice over his shoulder made him jump. "The Lost Collection... the highest form of honor or respect. A place for all those lost souls to be immortalized forever with the one who took their lives. Fitting, don't you think?"

Elliott turned to him with a look of horror, but even before that he realized that the doll in his hand was dressed the same as Marty, down to the battered purple backpack slung over this thin shoulder.

Marty stood regarding him coolly. In his hand was an absolutely enormous and sharp-looking knife. He had already stripped naked and was smiling perversely at Elliott.

Irrationally, Elliott pointed to the victims crowded into Marty's work-in-progress compartment. "But, where do you get those made from?" he asked.

As he stepped forward, bringing the knife up, Marty answered, "Well, you see... I'm not just a customer, I'm the President."

FREE TO GOOD HOME

"Oh my!" Richard Logan exclaimed as he looked at the squirming kittens in the cardboard box. "It's so hard to pick one, they're all so cute – I wish I could take them all." He would've clapped his hands for emphasis, but his hands were currently in the pockets of his cheap canvas jacket, where, like many animal lovers, there were treats: Pounce cat treats in the left-hand pocket and small Milk Bones in the right-hand pocket. Mr. Logan did not love animals.

He carefully considered the kittens in the box, a large mass of mewling, tumbling fur. Even though these kittens were all supposedly littermates – brothers and sisters – they didn't really look alike at all; two were ginger, another tabby-striped, and one poor bastard was just plain jet black. "Mr. Bad Luck," Logan said softly.

"Come again, mister?" The old lady with the long horsey face who had answered his call to the number listed in the paper under the boldface "FREE KITTINS" headline was looking at him expectantly.

Mr. Logan smiled widely and said, "Sorry, I was saying what a cute fellow little Blackie over here is," pointing to the black kitten, who was in the process of licking the doubtless worm-infested hindquarters of his ginger sibling. Logan smiled wider.

"You can pick em up, if you want," the lady said. "It's alright, the mama cat ain't around, I think she's out back sleepin' in the barn."

Given that these kittens barely had their eyes open yet, Mr. Logan doubted it. The only reason the mother would leave them at this stage would be to hunt. "That so? I bet! She must be real tired with all these little ones."

"Oh yeah," the horsey faced old lady said, smiling back at him. "When she's in the box, they won't give her a moment's piece, always at her, lookin' for some breakfast, I guess. And of course, the daddy cat – whoever he was – ain't around at all."

Logan shook his head sadly. "Just like a man," and they both laughed and he knew he could've had the box of kittens if he wanted them. A less experienced or less disciplined person might've been tempted to go for it, given that the only barrier was this homespun hillbilly housewife who just wanted to get rid of these kitties as soon as possible, but that might be a mistake, and, in this business, it did not pay to make mistakes.

Logan knew that was he was doing was technically "acquisition," but in reality, he was a salesman. His job was to evaluate what exactly would create a comfort level in a certain person, and then play to that note. Usually, he could glean enough from the preliminary phone conversation to figure out what would be the best tactic. Sometimes he was a lonely bachelor looking for a little furry companionship, and other times he sported the solid gold wedding band that sat ready in the white van's spotless ashtray.

Take this situation, for example. Mrs. Monroe, she of the long face and box of squalling kittens. Logan felt he could guess with almost 100% certainty a surprising number of factors about her life, just from the few minutes she had spoken to him on the phone and in this rural backyard. There was probably a husband, somewhere working, but not here. His typical rural view of animals, their place and their fate, much harsher than that of his urban and suburbanized counterparts, certainly not wanting to add a whole new litter of kittens, perhaps even offering to drown the babies in a sack. Mrs. Logan's tearful protestations, her promise to find the kittens a good home, "real quick."

That's why offering to take the whole box would be a mistake.

The motivation here was simple, Logan had seen it a thousand times before: to try and do the decent, humane thing for some helpless animals. If Mr. Logan said he wanted a kitten for himself, or his sweet little niece, or even his best friend Tyler who was unfortunately bedridden, this simple old woman would smile and understand and think nothing of it. If he said he wanted ALL of the kittens, she would nod politely, but inside, she'd be wondering – quite logically – what on earth he was going to do with a whole little of rambunctious kittens, and that would lead to questions, and questions were always best to be avoided.

And who knew? Perhaps in a few months the cat would have another litter, and there would be another grammatically amusing ad in the paper, and he could come back and get "a playmate for that wonderful kitten I got from you all before."

So, Logan smiled and listened to her prattle on for a few minutes, and when it came time to make his choice, he took one of the ginger ones, leaving the little black one to make his own luck.

He knew her offer of a cardboard box to transport his new acquisition was going to come next. He always kept a cardboard box of his own with a small piece of flannel inside it ("it gives them something to cuddle with!") so he could quickly secure the animal on the passenger seat until he was safely far enough away to make the change to one of the cages in the soundproof back of the van. They always offered a box, just like the lonely older ladies offered a cup of tea.

"Thank you again for coming out here, Mr. Logan," the horsey face said, strangely shy now. "I have a question to ask you, one that might seem a bit odd."

Inwardly, Logan frowned. Odd requests, like questions, like anything that deviated from his script, were to be avoided. Outwardly, however, he radiated sunshine and happiness. "What might that be, Mrs. Monroe? If you're going to ask me to mow the lawn, I am afraid I am a bit on in years for that job."

She laughed, as he knew she would, and looked at him for a moment with such a gaze of naked intensity that he almost took a step back. Was she going to mention PETA?

"I know you're a busy man, and probably want to get back to town with your new kitty, but I was hoping you could indulge an old woman – a lonely old woman – and come inside and share a cup of tea with me." She coquettishly glanced down at her feet. "I promise I won't keep you long."

Logan relaxed, and ruefully made a note of his paranoia. Like most people who are involved in shady activities targeting their fellow citizen, Logan was much more concerned about those folks than the police. A cop, say, stumbling upon Mr. Logan leaning over a fence and scooping a small white poodle while its owners were otherwise occupied, or perhaps snatching a black lab puppy from an SUV double-parked while the owner ran into the grocery store to get a quick item or two, that cop could conceivably arrest him on a misdemeanor charge, which, given his lack of criminal record, would mean an annoying court appearance, possible probation, and probably a fine – along with disastrous publicity. If the owners, on the other hand, were to do the same stumbling... well, some things were better left unimagined.

Unimagined, but certainly not unplanned for. Logan was proud of the elaborate contingency plans he had constructed. Of course, the best contingency plan of all was to assess a situation and avoid any possible complications. For Mr. Logan, that meant being alert for the bete noire of his existence – the crazy animal lovers.

It used to be just PETA nuts and the Animal Liberation Front kooks who did crazy shit like blowing up tuna boats because they accidentally snared a couple of dolphins in the process of commercial fishing, but lately it seemed that the crackpots were springing up more and more in mainstream places – having "playdates" for their puppies and invite-only birthday parties. Mr. Logan smiled at the thought of a kitty birthday party.

He was interrupted in his ruminations by the hopeful, expectant gaze of Mrs. Monroe. No paint-throwing animal activist here, just a lonely old lady who probably didn't even have that working husband – just her and her kitties against the world. Normally, he liked to get back on the road and get the delivery to the lab ASAP, but, sometimes rules were made to be broken.

"Well, normally..." he began, and seeing the crestfallen look on her horsey face ("Why the long face, Mrs. Monroe?" almost made him laugh out loud) decided him against his usual protocol. "I meant to say, I usually don't want to take up the time of such a charming young lady, but I have to say, you sure talked me into it. Only a quick cup though."

Mrs. Monroe brightened immediately. "Oh, thank you, thank you thank you! As I said, I promise not to keep you long."

She turned and headed across the yard to the old house. Logan spared a look back into the box of kittens; where his new acquisition was wrestling enthusiastically with one of its litter-mates – little needle teeth nipping away. "Enjoy it while you can," he thought. "This time tomorrow, you will be helping the field of science in ways you never imagined." As would the two puppies, one older border collie who formerly had tags that identified him as "Ranger" and the nervous boxer who were all currently quartered in the dark, air-conditioned environs of Mr. Logan's windowless van.

Business was good.

Well, maybe not as good as it used to be. With the race to develop and bring new products to market, the field for animal test subjects was a very lucrative one indeed. Most of the big firms these days used animals bred specifically to be research subjects, which was quite different from the old days, when Mr. Logan used to supply everyone from major pharmaceutical companies to the multinationals creating new soaps, shampoos and deodorants for consumers. In those halcyon days, he had a whole staff and fleet of vans providing a constant stream of four-legged product testers.

Of course, the ridiculous "animal rights" people put an end to that. So what if a microchipped family pet ended up being tracked to a university lab testing the effects of battery acid on skin? Was that supposed to be his fault? Everyone had quotas – the university lab, Mr. Logan's service, his staff. Sometimes thinking outside the box was required. Like the hypocrites at the labs and companies who pretended they didn't know where the bewildered, and frightened yet obviously very well-cared for research subjects came from.

Mr. Logan shook his head ruefully as he followed Mrs. Monroe across the sunny expanse of the yard. So, the days of the fleet and the staff were gone, replaced by just Mr. Logan himself, criss-crossing the country for a few "no questions asked" operations. The pay was still pretty good, and there was always the thrill of the hunt to keep him going. Yeah, there were a few die-hard competitors who traveled the same circuits and read the same want ads and were responsible for the same missing pet notices as Mr. Logan, but at least, unlike some of those individuals, at least he didn't hate the animals, he didn't needlessly abuse them. It was all a business for him.

He was a professional.

"You'll have to forgive things, it's a bit messy," Mrs. Monroe apologized. "I don't usually have a lot of visitors." She said as she led him through the back door and into the kitchen.

Blinking to adjust his eyes to the gloom, Mr. Logan revised his earlier guess about a husband – this domicile was strictly the work of one individual's unfettered eccentricity.

The interior of the house was clean, but every available surface was covered with some knick-knack, every wall had a poster – there was no open space.

And the subject of each knick-knack, of each poster? What the Humane Society of the United States refers to as "companion animals."

Galloping dogs cavorted from laser-photo calendars, ceramic kitties were tangled up with ceramic balls of yarn, images and effigies of birds, fish and all sorts of various little rodents were strewn everywhere. Logan was too overwhelmed to be unsettled by the sight before him. Even as he goggled at room after room of Precious Moments Schnauzers peacefully coexisting with Beanie Baby Siamese cats, at a calendar turned to August 1987 showing a striped angel fish next to an impossibly bright mechanical canary sitting with its head perpetually cocked inside a gilded cage, he didn't feel alarmed. This was no PETA covert operative; this was just a very strange old lady.

"Tea?" she said, holding out a steaming mug in front of Logan, and he jumped in spite of himself. She smiled indulgently as he absentmindedly accepted the mug. "I see you've all my pieces – I guess you could say I'm a collector." She gave a little self-conscious laugh. "I love animals, but I can't keep any." She solemnly placed a forefinger against her nose. "Allergies, you see."

Logan took a quick gulp of his tea. All this animal-themed clutter was making him a bit claustrophobic. Better to take a couple of polite sips and be on his way. "Of course, allergies." He took another sip of the tea, and looked in vain for a place to set down the mug. "This is very impressive, but I really must be..."

As if she didn't even hear him, Mrs. Monroe pointed at a cookie jar shaped like a St. Bernard. "Some nice fellow told me that Boris over there was a worth over a thousand dollars. Can you imagine! A dog cookie jar! I told him I'd never part with it, though. I traveled all over to get these pieces, and I love each and every one."

Mr. Logan was staring at a calendar photo of three albino bunnies. Their serious, pink eyes seemed to sit in judgment of him. Finally, he was starting to get the willies. He drained the last of his tea and squeezed the mug down next to one of those dippy birds that somehow seem to be drinking from a glass. Leaning against a table, a poster caught his eye. There were no animals on this one, it was more like a playbill, written in vaudeville era print, the headline said, "ONE NIGHT ONLY: THE AMAZING MISS CIRCE – FORTUNES TOLD, MINDS READ AND SECRETS REVEALED!!!" There was more to read, but it was starting to get uncomfortably warm in the crowded room.

"Ah, yes," Mrs. Monroe said from behind him, but this time Mr. Logan didn't jump. "I see you found one of my old advertisements. Probably a bit vainglorious of me to keep them around, but they remind me of my travels, where I was able to get lots of pieces – on the road. Kind of like you, you know, on the road, traveling."

Mr. Logan started to say something, but at that moment his legs gave way and he slumped to the floor, looking up questioningly at Mrs. Monroe. "Of course, I wasn't a kidnapper, I was just an entertainer." She nodded disapprovingly at Logan. "Really, separating people from their beloved companions! That's very naughty indeed. You really ought to be ashamed of yourself."

Logan started to raise a hand, but then a burst of such excruciating pain tore through his arm that he let out a surprised hiss. Another screaming spasm tore through his back, and all he could do was roll himself onto all fours. He looked up at Mrs. Monroe, who was gazing at him sadly.

"I know it's painful, I am really very sorry about that." She was daintily picking up his tea mug and wiping it out with a dishcloth. "I hate to see any creature in pain. But," she said, lifting the mug in a little salute, "as they say, you have to break a few eggs to make an omelet."

"Don't you worry," she said, reaching out a hand to pat his head gently. "The pain is only a brief side-effect, it won't last long, I promise."

Logan shook his head. She must've given him some hallucinogen in that tea. How else could he explain his right forearm, which was now a foot shorter than his left? His very fingers seemed to be collapsing in on themselves. He groaned and collapsed onto his side.

"The change is always painful, but it is an unavoidably important part of your education." Mrs. Monroe said absently, as she dialed a number on her telephone. She politely covered the receiver and stage whispered to him, "You know, some people say we're constantly reincarnated as higher life forms, so you don't have anything to worry about – if that's true, you should be back on two legs in no time at all." She frowned severely at him, the way one does to a puppy who has just piddled on the carpet. "I just hope you've learned your lesson. Well, if not now, perhaps soon. After all, I did promise I wouldn't keep you long."

She turned her back to him and began speaking quietly into the telephone. Mr. Logan felt himself receding down a darkening hallway. Even worse than the pain blaring from every one of his joints was the maddening itching of his face. He pawed at his cheeks but to no avail. The last thought he had, he could swear he felt whiskers sprouting.

"My, he's certainly a frisky one!" The man exclaimed, looking at the tiger-striped cat furiously clawing at the inside of the cardboard box. He smiled a wide grin at the old woman. "I can see why you say he's a bit too much for you to handle."

"Yes," she said sadly. "I hate to give him up, but I know you said you'd see to it he has a good home."

If possible, the man smiled even wider. Behind him, a nondescript blue van idled under the blue sky of the large yard. "You can sure bet on that!" he said, and they both laughed.

The man quickly folded down the corners of the box and turned, carrying it toward the van. He hummed a tuneless melody as he walked.

"Oh, mister?" The old lady called from the front porch.

"Yes?" he turned, smiling a trifle warily. Sometimes they had second thoughts. The last thing he needed was a tearful scene with this old biddy. He still had quite a few acquisitions to make today.

"I get lots of critters here, you should come back soon, and I'll have something else for you."

The man's original wide smile returned. This pickup had been a piece of cake. "You know, I just might do that."

The old lady returned his smile genuinely. "I really hope you do."

DROWNING IN THE SEA OF LOVE

"Three hundred and fifty dollars," Katie thought. "Three hundred and fifty dollars and nothing more."

All around her was a whirlwind of frenetic activity as technicians scurried around: A thin balding man wearing round eyeglasses was taking a reading with a light meter; another man smoking a clove cigarette was consulting a clipboard; a young fat man in a madras shirt and shorts that unfortunately showed off his pale and fleshy white calves who was doing pretty much nothing remarked to no one in particular: "Ugh. I ate a whole pizza for lunch and I can feel my pores actually *sweating* cheese."

The man holding her elbow and escorting her through the room smiled widely and said, "Welcome to the wonderful world of show business."

"Three hundred and fifty dollars and nothing more," Katie thought.

When Katie realized she needed to do something to get some money quickly, she turned to the ads in the back of the free weekly, and decided to answer the one that seemed the least creepy, which read: "WANTED. Pretty, clean young ladies for lucrative modeling assignments. You be pretty and clean (no fatties or intravenous) and we'll be professional and respectful to your limits." And, then, the one sentence that catapulted this ad from the level of complete creepiness (although what did they man by "no intravenous?") to definite interest: "Same day payday."

Katie called the number listed, and after confirming Katie was indeed over eighteen and had the requisite governmentally issued proof of same, the woman who answered gave Katie an address and a time and hung up.

After getting off the bus, Katie walked to the address, took a deep breath, pulled the door open and marched inside. Katie found herself in an exceptionally small reception area, consisting of two plastic chairs and a glassed-in window like at the currency exchange, behind which sat a young man so deeply engrossed in reading, he didn't even look up when Katie came through the door. Through the walls, Katie could hear the sounds of men working – hammering, large items shifting, the beep-beep-beep and whine of a forklift backing up – which seemed more suited to the inside of a Home Depot than a same-day-payday modeling agency.

"Um, excuse me, I'm here about the modeling?"

The young man still did not look up from his magazine. "That so? You have an appointment?"

"Yes, 9:30 a.m., I know it's a little early…"

The young man cut her off, opening the window and handing over a clipboard. "Fill out this application and when you're done attach your ID and bring it back to me," which was delivered all in one breath without his raising his gaze from the magazine, which Katie now saw was *Screenwriter's Monthly*.

"Than you, sir," she said politely, and this caused the young man to look up startled from an article on "Rising Action and CGI: 10 Things You Need to Know." He did a comical double-take and gaped at Katie for a few moments. Finally, he seemed to find himself and stuttered out, "Um, hold on a sec, wouldya?" Picking up a phone, he dialed two numbers and then said, "Um, Mr. Lomax, there's someone out here I think you should see." He paused for a moment and Katie could hear a loud voice, not shouting exactly but loud, through the receiver. "Uh, no, sir, not a process server. Uh, I think you'll see what I mean when you talk to her."

"Come on, I'll buzz you in," the young man said, gesturing toward a door.

Through the door and she followed the young man down a narrow hallway. Boxes and boxes of VHS tapes and DVDs lined the walls, all with lurid covers Katie deliberately didn't look at too closely. Past several small offices the young man pointed at a doorway at the end of the hall. The door was slightly ajar, and Katie could hear some more not-quite-shouting coming from within. "This is as far as I go," the young man said.

For a moment Katie was alone, and her nerve almost failed. She looked between that slightly ajar door and the one that led back to the street. Only the length of a small hallway of a building in some corner of an industrial park somewhere, but Katie thought it was more like a span of the known universe.

With a long sigh, she walked forward and knocked softly on the door, which opened a bit more, revealing a man standing up talking on the telephone behind a large cluttered desk. Cradling the phone between his right ear and his neck while lighting a cigarette, his eyes momentarily widened when he saw Katie, but only momentarily. He motioned her in the room and toward a chair in front of the cluttered desk while never interrupting his steady stream of verbiage, which drifted over Katie like a maddeningly incomprehensible foreign language:

"He what? He didn't! Arrgh, alright, put him on. Yes, I know very well how much a half day's rental of the stable is. Put him on." Pause. "Hi Buck, how's it going? Yeah, I bet you know why I'm talking to you. Do you know how much money you are costing me? Let me go over this one last, final time, Buck. What are we paying you for, and if you say "acting" I am gonna have Lefty break your leg. Right, we're paying you for a pop shot. How much are we paying you for the pop shot, that one little thing? That's right, Buck. That's a lot of money for one little thing. Now, what's the name of this production, Buck? Right again! 'Chin Omelettes 6!' And what do you think the discerning consumer who purchases a title called 'Chin Omelettes 6' wants to see? A chin omelette? Very good! Now, tell me what use is a pop shot of the girl's chest, over her head entirely or, worst of all, all her hair, when the title of the production is 'Chin Omelettes 6?' Right! No use! No fucking use at all! Now, there's the big money question, Buck, so pay attention: What use is the dumb fucking lummox who can't get a pop shot – the one thing and one thing only he is being paid to do – is the right place on film? I'm sorry, I didn't hear that? Right! No use at all. Do I make myself clear?

Alright. Look, if you have a trajectory problem, just aim at the collarbone, you'll do fine. OK? OK. Go drink a Red Bull and get back to work, and don't let Danny have to call me again."

The man abruptly hung up the phone and turned his attention to Katie. "Yeah, I can see why Tommy wanted me to talk to you. You're over eighteen, right? You got four forms of ID, all government issued?"

Hesitantly, she help up her hand, listing the contents, "Nooo... I don't, I just have a driver's license, a copy of my birth certificate, and my Nine West preferred customer card, do I need four?"

The man shook his head, "Naw, nobody I know has four forms of fucking government ID, unless they're a Fed. I'm Freddie Lomax, ringmaster of this here circus. Hand over your bona fides and answer a question for me: You're a pretty girl, you don't seem overly fucked up, tell me why on Earth you wanted to get involved in this."

"Well, Mr. Lomax, I really need the money."

Without looking up from the form he was copying Katie's information onto, Lomax said, "I see." Mr. Lomax paused, and Katie saw he had filled out all of the form except for one line, the "NAME" section at the top. He followed her gaze. "Yeah, I was wondering what we should call you."

Katie was happy to finally be prepared for a question. "Buttons Highway 5."

"Buttons Highway 5?"

"Yes."

Mr. Lomax sighed, a much longer one than Katie had allowed herself. "That's very good. Let me guess, your first pet and the street you lived on when you were little?"

Katie nodded, a bit uncertainly. Lomax shook his head slowly. "Buttons Highway 5. Jesus Christ." He stared into space for a moment in the direction of a push-pin filled wall map of the United States with the word "DISTRIBUTION" printed over it. "How about Tracey Nevada?" You got objections to that?"

Katie didn't think it was much better than her suggestion, but she nodded.

"Alright, Tracey. That's out of the way. Do you know what you wanna do for us?"

Katie blushed again. "No, not really."

Far from exasperated, Mr. Lomax seemed to be expecting that response. He pulled out a mimeographed sheet from his desk and uncapped a black Sharpie. "This is a call sheet of productions we currently have in progress – how about this, tell me what you won't do, and we'll work backward from there."

Katie paused. "Well, I don't want to do anything that my brother would find out about."

Lomax paused and then nodded sarcastically, "Of course, and this brother, I don't suppose he's ever been on the Internet, right?"

"Look, Mr. Lomax, this is really, really hard for me. If I didn't need the money more desperately, I wouldn't even be here. All my brother and his friends do is to smoke pot, play Playstation, and surf the net for porn. Hopefully, he and his friends would never find out about this, but I'd like to make it that way as much as possible. Oh, and no sex."

"I see, Lomax said, and looked at her speculatively. Then, with another long sigh, he bent over the list and began drawing thick black lines through items. He had crossed off about 70% of the titles when the phone buzzed and budding screenwriter receptionist voice came over the intercom, "Mr. Lomax, Teddy Field from Professional Modeling International is on line one, returning your urgent call."

Lomax handed Katie the paper. "Here, I have to take this call. Look this over and see if anything there looks probable." Without waiting for an answer, he picked up the phone and immediately began shouting.

Katie blocked out the booming voice and considered the few remaining titles on the sheet. Much like the earlier conversation she had overheard, it seemed to be made up of some secret language that she was not privy to. *Spank me spank me spank me!* seemed unappetizing but straightforward enough, but who were *Fisted Angels* anyway? And *Cameltoe Cuties* didn't seem any clearer. And she didn't even want to ask what *Cleveland Steamer Surprise* was all about.

Near the bottom of the page, there was a title crossed out, and handwritten in was *Drowning in the Sea of Love*. Kate was dubious about the whole "Sea of Love" part, but it sure sounded better than "Cleveland Steamer."

Mr. Lomax was still shouting into the telephone. "...and I'm telling you, the next time you tell me you're sending over a girl for "Bad Bad Teen Babysitters" and the girl turns out to be a Toyota Cressida station wagon-driving mother of two in pigtails who voted for Reagan not once, but TWICE, I am through with you!" Bam! He slammed the phone down again. "Did you find something?"

"Well, I thought this one looked possible, but I have to admit I am not quite sure what exactly it's about."

Lomax looked at what Katie had circled on the list. "What a coincidence, that production is shooting a scene this afternoon. I can explain to you while we go to the set. If you sign the paperwork, I'll get you your pay, this gig pays $300." He stopped and considered Katie's long blond hair. "$350 if you wear pigtails."

Mr. Lomax shouted through three more phone calls on the way over to the shoot, but Katie was thinking more about the $350 in cash he had given her, with the admonition not to ever tell anyone he had fronted her money.

They had barely walked through the door of a small, split-level Colonial when Lomax began screaming an older man carrying a tripod. "What the fuck are you doing wearing golf spikes on this wood floor, Clarence? Are you fucking crazy?"

The older man, apparently a veteran of Mr. Lomax's outbursts, didn't even beak his stride. "Chill out, man. I got a tee time in 45 minutes and I don't have time to change. As soon as I get this lighting set up, I am outta here."

"Watch out for the cables!" Lomax shouted at his retreating back. He took in the bustle of activity. "Troy! Troy, come here, I want you to meet someone."

A muscular young man wearing a sleeveless "Tool" t-shirt and drinking Super Big Gulp came over. He was cute, Katie thought, in a sort of Trans-Am driving, Milwaukee's Best-drinking kind of way.

"Troy – I mean Johnny! How's it going? I want you to meet who you're going to be doing the scene with this afternoon. This is Tracey Nevada. Tracey, this is the famous Johnny Gallon."

By way of greeting, he looked over Katie and said, "Too bad this is *PF12* and not *Gangbang Facepainters.*

"*PF12*?" Katie asked.

Mr. Lomax steered her away from the young man. "Um, Tracey, that's something I forgot to tell you. Lots of times, we use shorthand names for our productions in-house. So, uh, don't be surprised if people refer to this production by other than its release name, *Drowning in the Sea of Love*. Like, for example, someone may refer to *Pee Faces Twelve*, but that's just shorthand, ok?"

Katie opened her eyes. She was wearing a terrycloth robe and sitting in a large Jacuzzi bathtub. In a few minutes they were going to shoot her scene, of which her part consisted entirely of sitting naked in the tub while Johnny Gallon urinated on her.

"Three hundred and fifty dollars and nothing more," Katie said to herself.

Even with all the lights heating up the bathroom, the coldness of the tub still seeped through the robe and gave Katie chill bumps. She would get through this. Mr. Lomax had told her so. Mr. Lomax had told her a lot of things.

Mr. Lomax told her the there was absolutely no sex involved in this production, it just consisted of people peeing on other people, and people being peed on. Mr. Lomax said some folks – an increasing number of folks, he noted appreciatively – just wanted to watch people peeing on each other and were willing to pay premium prices for the privilege. Mr. Lomax said that, unless Katie's brother or his friends were among those seriously fucked up people, the chances were slim that they would ever stumble upon this production. Perhaps, most importantly, Mr. Lomax told her she would get paid $350 for about five minutes of actual work. "You don't even have to speak," he said.

"Places!" called the Assistant Director, and people began crowding into the bathroom, which was packed with lights, cables, and equipment. Johnny Gallon nosily slurped the last few drops of liquid out of his Super Big Gulp with a straw.

Katie looked at the faces of people crammed into the bathroom. In additional to Johnny Gallon, there was the AD who was opening the camera, Mr. Lomax, the director – a skinny man with a John Waters mustache who smoked clove cigarettes constantly and spoke with a German accent – and a lighting technician who also was holding a towel and a glass of water for Katie.

The director looked skeptically at Katie. "You sure about this, Freddie? The girl looks awfully green."

Lomax shouted back at him, "She'll be fine! This is going to be the best debut in watersports since *Tinkle, Tinkle Little Star!* You ready, Tracey?"

Katie nodded. Johnny Gallon took his place, standing fully clothed on the ledge of the tub, his crotch a few inches above Katie's pigtails. "Jesus, I gotta piss something fierce, let's go!" he said, and unzipped his jeans.

Katie pulled off the terry cloth robe and threw it to the PA. "Just like warm water, warm water for $350," she thought.

Now, if it hadn't rained steadily and uncharacteristically in Southern California for two days previously, there might not have been such a terrible loss of life on the set of *Pee Faces 12.* But, unfortunately, over six inches of rain had fallen in the last 48 hours.

As such, the new golf course at the former site of El Toro Air Base was waterlogged, and players were advised to use their extra long spikes for better traction on the greens. Clarence, who admittedly was lazy and hated the Southern California traffic as much as he loved pounding the ball around the links at a discount rate, had to reschedule a tee time to take advantage of the early bird twilight special and thusly had cut it so close, he changed into his golfing attire – including golf shoes – while still setting up the lights for Katie's scene. Since his long spikes were metal, not plastic like the smaller green spikes, and he was in a hurry, he never noticed that he punctured the protective rubber tubing on several of the long, thick cables snaking through the bathroom.

Furthermore, since Mr. Lomax didn't believe in shooting simply with a handheld video camera, but actually employed a camera operator and a director AND a PA, there were, not counting Katie, five other individuals crammed into the bathroom, a bathroom that had only one exit.

So, naturally, when Katie felt the firm warm stream of urine cascade across her face, she did what almost any young woman would do, and she screamed and closed her eyes and flailed her arms. Her right hand, including her high school class ring with its brilliant sapphire stone shout out, connected with the swollen testicles of the aptly named, "Johnny Gallon," causing him to yelp in pain and skid off the ledge of the bathtub, landing half in and half out of the tub, with the most unfortunate luck of his still voiding penis aiming a steady stream of urine at the snake box of cables.

Like a flicker of flame inexorably following an errant trail of gunpowder in an old Tom & Jerry cartoon, a spark leapt from one of the compromised cables and sent 550 volts of pure juice shooting back into Johnny Gallon's pecker, causing him to become, in less than one second, Johnny Screaming Human Torch.

Because Johnny was now a supercharged conductor instead of urine, he was dealing death out of his urethra. If the AD had been filming a 3-D production, he couldn't have asked for a better shot than the stream of crackling electricity coming straight at his camera lens. Alas, since he certainly had forgotten to ground himself, within seconds the camera had fused to the side of his rapidly melting face, which caused him to tumble into the director, who was yelling something unintelligible in German while apparently trying to run the through the bathroom's west wall. But, as anyone with a sixth grade science education knows, electricity travels through just about everything, including rapidly melting AD cameramen and Prussian porn directors. As the current surged through him, his jaw clamped shut, biting off the tip of his tongue, which fell to the floor jumping and sizzling like a piece of bacon in a hot skillet.

Mr. Lomax, with the wily instincts of a true survivor, had miraculously leapt up on the toilet at Katie's first scream, and was therefore able to avoid being barbecued with the rest of his crew. However, in a twist of extremely bad luck, the PA who was holding Katie's robe and towel was also holding a glass of water for her. When the runaway current jumped from the still-smoking corpse of the director and ran up the leg of the PA, the water glass in his hand blew up like a grenade, sending a fist-sized piece of Crate & Barrel's finest stemware directly into Mr. Lomax's left eye socket. This rather unexpected and unforeseen development caused him to pinwheel wildly on the toilet seat, as he exuded a mighty self control to keep from toppling onto the certain death of the sparking floor.

Unfortunately, while the owners of the split-level Colonial

had used some of the money they made renting out their house to skin flick producers on buying fine stemware, they skimped on the bathroom items, and their toilet seat was strictly Home Depot's cheapest, and, the tilting force of Mr. Lomax caused the cheap plastic rivets holding the seat on the toilet to snap like small twigs and send him to the aftermentioned certain death.

Electricity is an amazing thing. In less than seventeen seconds, five human beings had been reduced to small, smoking lumpy piles. The mischievous current looked around for more damage to cause, but, again, as any elementary age science student can attest, electricity seeks to complete a circuit, and so, after racing across the bathroom, the current shot back in the snake box, blowing it to smithereens and shorting out the local power grid for a six-block radius.

Some people would find it ironic, with all the old wives' tales about curling irons, blow dryers and even toasters frying people in bathtubs, that the Jacuzzi where Katie had crouched to avoid being peed on should be the one safe place, the one oasis, in that perfect storm of electricity.

And yet, when Katie cautiously opened her eyes, she was indeed the only living being in the split-level Colonial. Her employer – like his crew – was a steaming cinder on the floor. Her co-star, with one leg on each side of the tub, looked like a rodeo cowboy skeleton without the hat and with a little more burned flesh.

Gingerly, she stood up and surveyed the damage. The power outage had knocked out the lights, but by the warm glow of the PA's still burning body she was able to navigate her way out of the bathroom and find her clothes in the master bedroom. Outside, she could hear excited voices running down the street and sirens wailing by, doubtless chasing down one of the many burning transformer boxes in the subdivision.

Katie shook her head sadly. This kind of thing was always happening to her. Poor Mr. Lomax, but at least he paid her up front. She felt the comforting bulk of the cash in her front pocket. "Three hundred and fifty dollars and nothing more," she said.

The national best-selling author of ten acclaimed books – both fiction and non-fiction – **Jay Bonansinga** *is a rising star on the publishing and movie scenes. His novels have been translated into 9 different languages, and his 2004 non-fiction debut* The Sinking of the Eastland *was a Chicago Reader "Critics Choice Book" as well as the recipient of a Superior Achievement Award from the Illinois State Historical Society. His debut novel* The Black Mariah *was a finalist for a Bram Stoker award, and his numerous short tales have been published in such magazines as* Amazing Stories, Grue, Flesh & Blood *and* Cemetery Dance, *as well as a number of anthologies.*

Jay also proudly wears the hat of indie filmmaker: his music videos have been in heavy rotation on The Nashville Network and Public Television, and his short film City of Men *was awarded the prestigious silver plaque at the Chicago International Film Festival. In 2006, his feature-film debut,* Stash *(based on the story of the same title collected here), goes before the cameras in Chicago. Jay is the holder of a master's degree in film from Columbia College Chicago, and currently resides in Evanston, Illinois, with his wife and two sons. He is also a visiting professor at Northwestern University in their Creative Writing for the Media program.*

ANIMAL RITES

Stirring awake, Daddy Norbert found himself tied to a moldy La-Z-Boy in the tool shed out back of the garage. Head felt like a rusty nail had been driven into it. Something sticky was digging into his belly. Would have rubbed his puss-bleary eyes, but he found his big calloused mitts hog-tied to the springs beneath him.

"Whylmmmphrump?" Daddy's query was sabotaged by stupid lips.

"Good!" The voice popped out of the shadows like a firecracker. "You're comin' awake."

"Illliihhsh?" Although Daddy's mouth was still asleep, his eyes were sharpening, beginning to make out a faint figure before him.

"Takes it a spell to wear off," the voice said.

Daddy Norbert blinked. "Lizzy...? That you?"

"Yessir."

"'The hell is going on?!'"

Stone silence.

Daddy Norbert blinked some more, and started putting things together. His teenage stepdaughter Lizabeth must have slipped him a Mickey back at the house and dragged him out here to the toolshed. Girl was seriously wrong in the head. Been that way ever since her mama died. Getting skinnier and skinnier, messin' with that faggotty colored boy up to Little Rock.

Now the girl must've gone stark raving screwy. Crouching in the shadows across from Daddy, fiddling with something that sounded like a tin cup with a nail in it. Girl was crazy as a crosseyed loon.

"Almost ready," the voice finally said. "Just hold your horses."

"What in the wide friggin' world of sports is going on?!"

"Be still."

"What did you slip me, girl?"

"Called Tranxene. It's temporary, so just shut up and sit still for a minute."

"Don't you sass me!"

Skinny little bitch didn't even react, just kept on working with that rattling box of metal. Daddy's eyes were adjusting to the dark. He could see strips of old duct tape wrapped around his massive girth. Something leather was holding his head in place like blinders on a plough horse. Smelled like wet dog fur.

Daddy swallowed hard. "Lizzy, why you doin' this?"

"It's a secret."

"Whattya mean, secret?"

"You'll see."

"I'm sorry," he told her all of a sudden. His bowels were beginning to burn, his mouth going dry as wheat meal. It was dawning on him, this girl could very easily hurt him. Maybe hurt him a lot. "I'm sorry for what I did to you and your mama. You hear me? I'm tellin' ya how sorry I am."

No answer.

"Lizzy?"

She switched on the light.

The sudden glare of an old aluminum scoop light exploded across the shed. Blinking fitfully, Daddy saw the shriveled carcasses splayed across his work bench to his left. His future projects. Parts of a rabbit, a young fox, the hind end of a bobcat. Rusty traps were arrayed across the walls. Behind him, mounted on a shim of hardwood, a deer looked on, its lifeless eyes glimmering.

Daddy looked down at Lizzy and drew in a sudden breath.

She was on the floor, securing one of Daddy's favorite guns, a custom Roberts rifle, into a weird contraption of metal and wood. Looked like a spring loaded skeet shooter. The rattling sound that Daddy had heard must've been the bullet. Lizzy was loading a .219 Zipper into the gun's chamber. The Zipper was Daddy's favorite brand. A 90-grain, heavy powder compression load, the bullet would take down an adult elk bull at two hundred yards.

The barrel of the rifle had a bead drawn right smack dab on

Daddy.

"Now hold on, child!" Daddy Norbert started breathing hard, fighting his restraints, electric current shooting up his spine. Fear made his sphincter contract. "Yyyyyyyyyyyou ain't gonna shoot me, just simmer down now!"

"There," Lizzy said softly to herself, finishing the load as though she had just put a cake in the oven. She stood up and gazed at Daddy emotionlessly, her eyes rimmed in dark circles. She looked like a person who had just come home from a funeral. Drained and wrung out. She was holding a jury-rigged triggering device, the pull-string from an old push mower. It was tethered to the Roberts. Underneath Lizzy's sleeveless blouse, a tank top had the letters P.E.T.A. imprinted on it. People for the Ethical Treatment of Animals.

Daddy had never seen that before.

"Taste it?" she calmly asked him. "The fear?"

"Let-let-let-let-lllet go of that thing," Daddy stammered, "we can talk this out."

"Like the deer?" She bored her gaze into him. "You talk things over with the deer?"

"Wwwwwwaitwaitwaitwait! Just tell me wwwwwwwwhat you want me to do? You want me to say I'm sorry? I'm sorry! Awright? I'm sorry, I'm sorry, I'm sorry!"

Lizzy didn't answer. Instead, she closed her eyes, bowed her head, and began mouthing a secret litany. Daddy Norbert started to say something else, but he stopped abruptly when he saw the objects in her other hand. Lizzy was grasping a handful of objects twined together with string. Sprigs of herbs or weeds or some other kind of nonsense that her Jamaican boyfriend had probably given her. Strands of hair, human hair maybe. A silk ribbon, a bookmark from Lizzy's old Concordance bible, and some other strands of unidentifiable fabric. But none of it currently seemed as important, or made as much of an impression on Daddy Norbert, as the tiny black objects hanging from the bottom of the thing.

The broken beads of her dead mother's rosary.

"Hold the phone!" Daddy Norbert barked at her. "You ain't mad about no deer! You're still steamed about your goddamned ma! For God's sake, it ain't my fault she up and died! Already told you a million times, I'm sorry I hit her! You'd think I planted the goddamn cancer in her goddamn cervix myself! It weren't my fault! Now Lizzy, just stop it! STOP IT RIGHT NOW!"

Lizzy kept gazing at him.

"YOU SKINNY LITTLE HALFPINT, PUT THAT GUN AWAY 'FORE I GIVE YOU ANOTHER WHOOPIN'!!"

Lizzy gripped the cable and smiled. Her face was a rictus of pain. "This is for you, great white hunter," she uttered. It sounded rehearsed.

Then she pulled the cable.

"AAAAAAAHHHHHHHHHHHHHHH!!"

Eyes slamming shut, Daddy Norbert winced. Matter of fact, he winced so hard a little squirt of shit spurted from his anus. He thought he heard the pop. The sharp blast of the hammer hitting the pin, and the bones shattering in his face. But he must've imagined it. Actually, he felt nothing. Just the warmth in the seat of his pants and the painful throb of his heart.

He opened his eyes.

At first, he figured the gun must've misfired. There was a thin veil of smoke rising in the light, and Daddy thought he smelled the oily aroma of gunpowder. Lizzy was backing toward the door, her gaze still riveted to the man. What the hell was going on? Why was she looking at him like that?

"For you..." she whispered as she slipped through the door and into the cool Arkansas night.

"What the?" Daddy looked down at the gun and studied it for another moment. The black hole of its barrel was staring at him, the smoke diffusing, the silence like a block of ice over Daddy's head. Daddy blinked again and suddenly there were tears in his eyes. All at once, he realized just how lucky he really was. "I'll be a sonofabitch," he muttered, grinning to himself in spite of his frayed nerves. "Twenty-three years in the woods, and not one dud, and tonight the goddamned thing decides to misfire!"

He began to giggle.

"I'll be a swivel-hipped sonofabitch! Goddamned misfire! GOD DAMNED MISS-FUCKING-FIRE!! WHOOPTY-DO AND FUCK ME BLUE!!"

Daddy laughed and laughed and laughed, and then he looked down at the gun.

His laughter died.

Something had appeared in the mouth of the barrel. Something round. Just barely poking out, the light shining off it like a tiny planet. At first, Daddy wondered if it was an obstruction, an odd fragment of metal that had gotten wedged in there after a misfire during his last hunting trip. The thing looked familiar, the blue steel gleam winking in the dim light.

The .219 calibre Zipper.

"Holy fuckin' shit," Daddy uttered, staring at the bullet peeking out of the barrel. He'd heard stories of freak misfires, bullets getting lodged in barrels and such. But he never really believed them. Always figured it was whiskey talk, nothing more.

Grin widening, he closed his eyes. "Sweet Jesus, Lord in heaven, I realize I ain't been to church in a month of Sundays, but I wanna thank y'all just the same."

A chill breeze wafted in through the half-ajar door, and it cooled the beads of sweat on Daddy's forehead. He opened his eyes, grinning like an idiot. He could smell the surrounding farms, the sorghum, manure and wet hay. The odors never smelled so good to Daddy Norbert. He was alive, and that was all that mattered. Next step was to figure out how to get out of this fucking chair. Glancing down at the rifle, he took one last gander at the bullet.

His smile faded.

The bullet had moved, just a tad. Matter of fact, if Daddy Norbert was any less familiar with the shape of the Zipper's casing, he might have not even noticed. But there it was, poking out of the barrel, one, maybe two additional inches of casing. Daddy swallowed air. Maybe it was just a trick of the light, op'kil illusion or whatever you call it. He studied the muzzle of the Roberts and felt his heart flip-flop in his chest.

The bullet was half way out the barrel.

"Gotta have that damn thing checked." He chuckled softly. "Ain't that a kick."

Daddy stared at the rifle. If he didn't know better, he could have sworn the bullet had moved some more. Moved with the subtle steadiness of a clock. 'Course, that was impossible. That was damn near Mad Hatter crazy. He took a breath and tried to rip his arms free. The rope held tight. His fingers were going numb, and he could feel the mess in his pants, burning his butt crack, stinking to high heaven.

"Wait'll I get my hands on that skinny little – !

All at once, Daddy Norbert noticed the bullet was protruding nearly all the way out of the barrel now.

Defying gravity.

He blinked, and he blinked, and he blinked some more, and he still saw it. With his very own watery eyes. The Zipper was sticking almost clean out of the muzzle. Daddy wondered if a strange pocket of air had gotten trapped in the muzzle behind it... or something like that. Didn't really matter though, because the bullet was going to clear the lip of the barrel any second now and fall to the floor.

Except it didn't fall.

"What the fuck?"

Daddy gawked. Damn bullet hung in midair in front of the muzzle like a moth in aspic. No visible means of support. And Daddy got to thinking all of a sudden, thinking about Lizzy and that shit she was holding in her hand a minute ago and how she had that screwy look in her eye. Something cold and hard started turning in Daddy's gut. Chills rolled up his back, and the tiny hairs stood at attention along the back of his neck. The duct tape was digging into his belly. His head throbbed against its restraint. The worst part wasn't the fact that the bullet was frozen in space, which was pretty goddamned impossible if you thought about it for a second. Wasn't even the fact that it seemed to be slowly yet steadily inching forward.

The worst part was that it was heading straight for Daddy Norbert.

He frowned. The bullet was out of the muzzle by severalinches now, moving through the space between the gun and Daddy with the inexorable slowness of a sundial. It looked like a tiny grey stain in the air. Impossible. Goddamned impossible, but here it came. A two hundred calibre magic trick. Maybe six feet, seven at the most, between the bullet and Daddy. At this rate, it would take the bullet at least ten minutes to reach him. Then what?

Stupid thing would probably bump Daddy's nose and plummet to the floor like some second-rate levitation trick, like some throw-off from the Amazing El Moldo.

"Piece of shit parlor trick!" Daddy giggled again, his voice stretched thin. "Can't scare me with some cheap dime store gag!"

The bullet continued coming.

A scalding tear of sweat ran down Daddy Norbert's forehead and pooled in his eye. It burned. Daddy blinked, and cursed, and strained against the leather head restraints. He shook furiously against the tape. It was no use. Lizzy had done a bang up job on the bondage.

Daddy's cursing sputtered and died.

"This ain't possible," he uttered, his gaze glued to the bullet. Daddy Norbert had never really believed in magic before.

Growing up dirt-poor in the Ozark Mountains, he'd certainly run across his share of hokum. One old gal who lived behind the Norbert's pig farm was rumored to be a witch, but Daddy never believed it. Occasionally there'd be a gypsy clan who'd pass through the neighboring town. Some said it was gypsies that brought the drought of '49 to Pinkneyville. But Daddy never bought any of that hoodoo shit. Daddy Norbert was a simple hill-billy boy who grew up into a simple hillbilly man. Never got much of an education. Stayed out of trouble most of his adult life. Sure, he slapped his women around a little bit; he wasn't proud of it. But Jesus God, did he deserve this?

The bullet kept coming, crossing the half way mark now, hanging in the air just as horrible as you please.

Something snapped inside Daddy Norbert, as sure as a guil-lotine in his brain. Fear. It stole his breath and flowed cool through his veins. Stung his eyes. Made his fists clench up like vices until blood started soaking the ropes.

He'd been up against many a rough scrape in his day. Tangled with the Mueller boys down to Quincy. Got caught cheating at Anaconda on a river boat casino. Fought three cops on the side of the road once, got away with a single broken rib and a chipped tooth. But this was different, way over the edge; because all of a sudden Daddy realized this was what his own daddy used to call "bad juju."

The bullet crept closer.

"Okay, okay, okay, okay" Daddy started breathing deeply, try-ing to settle down, trying to convince himself it was all a trick, and that everything was going to be okay... but there was that shiny grey stain in the air coming right at him. And the leather binding holding his head in place. And the terrible certainty that

Lizzy and her colored buck had planned this thing especially for Daddy. And that the bullet's destination was somewhere in the vicinity of Daddy Norbert's forehead, just above his left eye. "Okay, okay, okay, okay, calm down, okay, get it together, calm down, calm down."

Daddy Norbert blinked.

Something sparked around the armature of the bullet. Sudden veins of light, erupting outward like the afterimage of a photographer's bulb. Faint lines mapping the darkness. A ghostly image curling around the zipper like a heat ray mirage cured in whiskey misted eyes –

(– *years ago, drooling drunk, his rough hands ona*
pale flesh, wedging himself inside a young girl's thighs, forcing himself into her, again and again, the sound of her smothered cries –)

"Wwwwhhha?!"

Daddy slammed his eyes closed."

The realization was like a claw hammer to his forehead.

Visions. He remembered his grand-mammy having visions of the end of the world, talking to Jesus in her sleep, and all of a sudden Daddy Norbert realized this was one of those kinds of visions. Daddy Norbert was having a vision of the end of the world. He was a sinner, he had done wretched things and now this was his very own reckoning day.

"Our father who, who, who, who art in heaven hallowed be thy name, thy, thy, thy SHIT!!"

Eyes popping open, Daddy saw that the bullet was less than two feet away now. So close, Daddy could see the serial number on its collar. He tried to swallow, but his spit was long gone. Throat like a lime pit. Piss spurting out of him. He didn't deserved this kind of hellish fate. A simple hillbilly, never got an education, never meant no harm, he just didn't deserve this. He began to cry. "GET IT OVER WITH! JUST DO IT! FINISH IT!!" His voice was like old metal tearing apart. "GET IT OVER WITH!!"

Twelve inches to go.

Another vision bloomed from the metal jacket. Veins of electric lightning threading out in all directions, coalescing into images, stormy images, apocalyptic images bombarding Daddy Norbert –

(– the snap of a belt on a woman's thick rear end, across the backs of her arms, drawing red streaks and welts... the red rain falling on parched ground, the locusts and the seven wax seals pealing away in the wind... the strangled cries of his wife, begging for mercy, mercy, no mercy –)

– until he shook the memories off like gasoline on his face and cried so hard his snot ran across his lips in salty

stringers. He prayed, and he bawled, and he begged God to come deliver him from this terrible trick.

Six inches now.

Daddy watched the bullet inching toward his forehead, his body convulsing with the fear and the tears and the shaking. The tape held him steady, the leather braced his head. Five inches. Four. Three.

"Our-father-who-art-in-h-h-h-h-h-h-h-h-h-heaven hallllll-hahhahhhh!"

The sudden flare of blinding light strangled off his voice.

He slammed his eyes shut and jerked backward with the force of the vision.

This time, the image was brutally clear.

(– Daddy was naked, hunched in a thicket of weeds in the forest, breathing hard, trapped...he could smell his own spoor, the warmth of his fur and the tympany of his heart...his hooves were split and bleeding in the leaves...his antlers ached, and he could see the glint of something shiny through the trees across from him, the barrel of a well seasoned Roberts rifle sticking out of the brush...then the flash of a .219 calibre shell exploding–)

At that moment, in the harsh light of the lonely tool shed, the cool metal tip of the bullet softly kissed Daddy Norbert's forehead just above the left eye...

...and kept coming...

...beginning Daddy Norbert's official – albeit long overdue – education.

STASH

Let's get the names out of the way:

- Douchebag
- El Douche
- Douchey-Douche
- Son of Douche
- Douche Junior
- The Douche Prince

These were the ones he remembered.

There were more, although he'd blocked most of them out of his memory. His gym teacher in the sixth grade, Mr. Blundy, called him Lil Douche, which, at the time, was as humiliating as any of the others, but over the years had kind of grown on him. Lil Douche has a certain hip-hoppy ring to it. Like an opening act for P-Diddy or Ol' Dirty Bastard. Or maybe the Massengil Summer Reggae Festival. All of which would be great, were he not the whitest dude you'll ever meet. A man without roots, without an identity.

A product of state orphanages, Guy Fox was adopted as a toddler and grew up in Caucasian Land (actually Grand Rapids, Michigan). He was weaned listening to the New Christy Minstrels and eating Bologna sandwiches slathered in mayonnaise. He went to an expensive Episcopalian prep school where the only black student was a light skinned Cuban boy named Pierre LaFontant whose blackest act was wearing a Sears Dashiki and playing Harry Belafonte's "Banana Boat Song" after lights-out. By the time Guy had made it to the University of Michigan, he was a full fledged honky motherfucker, from his Ivy League haircut down to his Izod chinos and top-siders. He looked like an ad for Eddie Bauer's "Young Republican Resort Wear."

Maybe that was why he eventually came up with the Porno Pal System. Maybe it was all about rebellion. Or maybe he wanted to do something "black." Something earthy and dangerous and subversive and cool.

Chances are, though, it was simply a way to thumb his lily white nose at his adopted dad.

"Where are you?" Guy snapped at his cell, gripping the phone tightly with one hand as he steered the car with the other. He was on the outer drive, skimming over parched pavement, heading north, preparing to clean up another mess in a home on the north shore of Chicago.

It was a gray September day, the sky low and skudded with dark clouds. To Guy's right stretched the endless mercurial waters of Lake Michigan, and to his left the canyons of cloistered condos known as Lincoln Park. Guy had both the air conditioning and a Korn CD blasting, and the cumulative din was making it hard to hear his partner.

"I'm almost there," the voice crackled. It belonged to Bobby Dutchik. Guy's Pal Friday since high school, Bobby made up for his room temperature IQ with a certain kind of sweetness that Guy had yet to encounter in any other straight, white, middle-class, horny males.

"Well don't do anything until I get there," Guy instructed, glancing at his watch. "It's not even 2:00 o'clock yet."

"Didn't the contract say the funeral was like from 1:00 to 4:00?"

"2:00 to 4:00," Guy corrected him.

"Sorry."

"Don't sweat it, I'll be there in a nanosecond. Just sit in your car, do some crossword puzzles."

Bobby assured Guy that he would do just that, and Guy disconnected the cell.

It took Guy a little over twenty minutes to find the address. Working off the contract, as well as the attached map, he located the huge Queen Anne at the end of a tree-shrouded street near the lake. Way upper class neighborhood. Cobblestones, mansions, security systems up the ying yang.

Guy parked his car a half a block away and strolled over to the client's wrought iron gate with his official-looking blue uniform shirt buttoned to the collar, and his official-looking clipboard tucked under his arm. It was standard work attire. Never failed to blend in. Guy was just some dude showing up to install a satellite dish or change a furnace filter. Rich people are used to this kind of crapola. On top of that, Guy Fox's physique had become about as non-threatening as a physique can be. Soft, pale, a little paunchy around the middle, he looked like an accountant or an actuary who'd been staring at so many spreadsheets, his own sheets had started to spread.

"Hey, G, you made it!" Bobby Dutchik called out as Guy approached the entrance gate. Bobby was leaning against the wrought iron fence in his own fake blue uniform, whistling absently, a tall, rangy man, his buggy eyes magnified by Coke bottle glasses.

"All set?" Guy said as he looked for the key pad that was supposed to be a few inches to the left of the gate's lock. Bobby said sure, everything was copacetic, as Guy consulted the contract for the proper code.

They opened the gate, strolled up the gorgeous herringbone brick sidewalk, and entered the house through the front door using the key that had been enclosed with the contract packet.

It's strange: When there's a death in a family, an empty home somehow seems to be more silent than your average empty home. Guy never mentioned this observation to Bobby – Guy wasn't even sure Bobby would get it – but Guy noticed it every time he entered a client's domicile. This house was no different. The front foyer was huge, with a soaring vaulted ceiling and sky lights, and as quiet as a Pharaoh's tomb. The rest of the house was straight out of Architectural Digest. Expensive furniture, meticulous decor. Lush greenery everywhere. Guy couldn't remember what the client's job had been: Heart surgeon? CEO? Something like that. It wasn't important.

They put on their surgical gloves and went about their business with minimal conversation or fuss. Guy kept the floor plan handy, and Bobby carried the canvas tent bag. (Over the years, they had learned through trial and error that plastic garbage bags are woefully ill-suited for this work; pornography can be heavy, and have sharp edges.)

On the second floor, at the end of the hall, as notated in the contract, they found the client's home office. The air smelled faintly of stale smoke and aftershave in there, and there was something vaguely poignant about the clutter. This was another thing Guy had noticed over the years: Old, white, rich, married men always have home offices, or rumpus rooms, or dens, or whatever, where they go to be alone. Maybe this was the secret to a happy marriage. A husband having a masculine place in which to retire after dinner each night, a place of dark leather uphol-stery and English fox hunt wallpaper within which a man can smoke a cigar and drink a Scotch and think deep thoughts about sports or cars.

This office was a prime example: The decedent's big oak desk was front row center, surrounded by golf trinkets, bowling tro-phies, model trains and framed prints of Norman Rockwell paintings. Behind the sofa, under a false floorboard, Guy found a cardboard file box full of *Hustler, Barely Legal, Screw, Beaver Hunt, Naughty Nymph, School Girl Pussy,* and *Awesome Asian Asses.* He carefully transferred the well-thumbed magazines to the canvas bag, and moved on.

The whole removal session took less than a half an hour. In the basement powder room, behind a cadenza brimming with photos of grandchildren, Guy removed a peach crate filled with dozens of videotapes, mostly fetish stuff, *Oriental Ass Reamers 17* and *Buttman Goes to College* Volumes 1 through 23. In the attic, nestled in the bottom of a moth-ball redolent trunk, underneath long forgotten sleeping bags and musty hunting gear, Bobby found vintage magazines and paperbacks with titles such as *The Big Suck-Off* and *Mona Takes a Pony Ride.* By the time they were done, the canvas bag was filled to the straining point. Bobby guessed it weighed at least a hundred and fifty pounds. Which was about right for a man who had lived a full life well into his seventies. A couple pounds of porno for every year. That was just about the norm, Guy had noticed: a magazine a month.

They made their final sweep, and everything looked good. They left the house just as they had found it.

On his way out the front door, Guy felt a wave of satisfaction rise through him. The day had turned mild, the sun burning off the clouds, and now the sky was high and blue over the north shore as he walked back to his car. But best of all: Guy had completed another job without incident. He had removed a deceased man's pornography promptly and professionally, before his wife or mother or daughter or granddaughter had a chance to stumble upon it and suffer mixed emotions about their dearly departed. Guy had discreetly cleansed a man's home, leaving behind nothing but Norman Rockwell, grinning grandchildren, and mothball perfumed trunks. And for the survivors, Guy had insured a period of simple, focused, undiluted, healing grief.

Grief without embarrassment.

"You going back to the office?" Bobby asked, tossing the canvas bag into his trunk. Bobby was supposed to stop at the dump incinerator on his way back to the shop, destroying all the smut – which Guy referred to in his company literature as 'retrieval materials' – in order to insure that no evidence would survive. But Guy was painfully aware that Bobby often stopped off at his apartment first to cherry pick whatever goodies might be of interest to him. He thought he was pulling a fast one on Guy, but Guy didn't care. Since becoming impotent a couple of years ago, Guy Fox couldn't begrudge a man his vices.

"Yeah, we got a customer coming in at 3:00 for a prospectus," Guy replied, glancing at his watch. "Then we got the Douche King coming over tonight for dinner."

Bobby cringed. "Ouch."

"Yeah, well... anyway... good job today, Bobby. I'll see you tomorrow."

"Seeya, Guy."

Guy walked the rest of the way to his car marveling at how fast a good mood can evaporate when his dad's name is invoked.

*   *   *   *   *

Guy's dad was indeed "The Douche King."

In fact, no less an authority than Fortune Magazine dubbed the elder Fox exactly that in a cover story in the late eighties.

When Guy was adopted in 1961–a former ward of the Department of Children and Family Services who would turn out to be his parents' only child–his father was in senior management at Parke-Davis Pharmaceuticals, working on new feminine hygiene products and being groomed for a top slot in the organization. But his masterpiece was the Daisy-Fresh. The world's first pre-mixed, pre-measured, non-allergenic disposable douche. The product was a blockbuster, bumping up the parent company's stock by a hundred and seventy-five bucks per share the first fiscal quarter alone, and alleviating women around the world of that not-so-fresh feeling.

Guy was only seven years old at the time this windfall came, and a seven year old former orphan with self-esteem problems is not exactly cognizant of all the financial implications of such success. Little Guy Junior only noticed three things: He saw less of his father; the family started eating out more often; and people at school started making fun of Guy. Maybe the experience hardened him. Looking back on it, he wasn't sure. But one thing was certain: It made him awkward with women. Hindered by the terrible knowledge that his dad–the man Guy saw each evening trimming his nose hairs and excavating toe jam–was in fact spending each day pondering vaginal odors, Guy was a complete disaster with girls.

He fared a little better in college–perhaps because of the widened proximity from his father–but still couldn't shake the Douche King curse. "Oh my God, that's where I heard your name before," they would intone as soon as Guy got them into bed. "Your dad's the douche guy. I'm wearing him right now. As we speak! I've got your dad inside me! Isn't that amazing? Your dad is in my vagina right at this moment! He's down there! Right now! He's there! Unbelievable."

Thank God Guy finally met Karen.

Karen was his savior–in a literal and religious sense. She was his Goddess. An English Lit geek at U of M, she was one of those girls with the skinny horn-rims and tattooed ankles who always seem like they're in on something that you aren't. Karen was the perfect girl friend because she had an aversion to toiletries of any kind. A hirsute girl, she let her armpits and legs go untrimmed, and eschewed all feminine hygiene products.

Guy and Karen were married a month after graduation, and moved to Chicago to look for actual jobs. Karen was the one with credentials that meant anything–a BA in English and a BS in

Special Education–and she landed a job right out of the gate at a prestigious private school on the Northshore called Blessed Virgin Mother Mary of the Universal Immaculate Conception. In her spare time, she crafted elaborate and morbid collages with the pictures of missing children cut from the sides of milk cartons. As for Guy: Let's just say his BA in 19th Century Icelandic Literature was not going to serve him in good stead at the Polo Club...unless he wanted to use his diploma to scrape smegma from the ponys' genitals. No, Guy Fox was destined for some-thing much more... shall we say... entrepreneurial.

Which was as good a way as any to describe the kind of work he was doing at this very moment in his modest little office on Sheridan Road.

"Tell me how it works," the gentleman was saying, sitting across the desk from Guy.

"Of course," Guy said, then pushed himself away from his battered veneer desk and walked around to the flip chart next to the window. The office was nothing special. Three hundred square feet of carpeted space in the rear of a two-bit ambulance chasing firm just north of Chicago. An outer room with a sofa and a few magazines. A couple of landscapes on the wall. Nothing too flamboyant. Nothing to make the customer uncomfortable. After all, The Porno Pal System was all about comfort. "It's really very simple," Guy explained, pointing to a color-coded flow chart emblazoned with big symbols such as $$$ and XXX and COD. "The first payment is an initial (non-refundable) one-time fee of $1500, plus a deposit of $5000. The deposit is contractually kept in escrow until you pass away or decide to cancel the contract for any reason."

The man in the arm chair, a gentleman named Herbert Cooley, was nervously nodding his head. Tall and gaunt and fidg-ety, with dishwater grey hair and skin so pale and wrinkled it looked almost translucent, he was obviously uneasy with this whole process. He looked to be in his 60's, although it was hard to tell for sure. He wore a short-sleeve shirt buttoned up to his shriveled Adam's apple, polyester slacks, and huge wingtips. He had dark circles under his eyes.

"How do you... know... the... um... location?" Cooley wanted to know.

"That's an excellent question," Guy remarked with an amiable smile, trying to put the elder man at ease. Guy had seen all types coming through this door – everybody from clergy to rap singers – and there was always this initial mixture of nervous tension and shame. "Along with the deposit, you submit floor plans of your house, along with a house key and the location of all the hiding places where the... uh... material is kept."

"I see," said Herb Cooley.

"These items are kept in a safe deposit box," Guy went on, pointing at a little illustration in the flow chart of a bank vault. "At your expense, of course, with explicit directions that the box should be opened only upon your death, and only by myself or my associate."

"Very good then," Cooley said with weird Anglo-style diction, wringing his gnarled hands, staring at Guy.

At that moment, with the abruptness of a synapse firing in the back of Guy's brain, he became certain of one thing: There's something wrong with this guy.

"Additionally, an addendum letter will be filed with your estate attorney," Guy was saying now, distracted by the gooseflesh rashing the back of his arms, "stating that my associate and I are from an historic preservation foundation, and we should be allowed to enter your domicile upon your death in order to collect some of the your – quote-unquote – important papers." Guy tried to smile and couldn't. "It's really just a formality. All of it completely legal."

Now it was Herbert Cooley's turn to approximate a smile, and the result was something that would haunt Guy's dreams from this day forward. The corners of Cooley's thin, liver-colored lips twitched, and his red-rimmed eyes widened, and his slack face pulled away from crooked yellow teeth as though a puppeteer's string were tugging at his deeply lined temples. "Where do I sign?" he softly intoned.

Guy's hands were shaking as he pulled open the drawer to fetch a contract.

* * * * *

An entire week passed before Guy finally acted on his suspicions. During that week, Guy went about his business in an orderly fashion, never letting on to anyone that he was being haunted by a major creep of a client. And the strangest part was, Guy had no proof of any irregularities. Cooley's deposit check had cleared, and his papers seemed to be in pristine order. There was no reason to believe that Cooley was anything other than a decent, red-blooded American user of pornography. The only thing that was eating at Guy was that one face-to-face. The incredible feeling during that meeting that Herbert G. Cooley was just... wrong.

But Guy kept this feeling to himself. Didn't even tell Bobby about it. Just kept it in the back of his brain where it festered like an abscess. This was a first for Guy. In the five years since he had founded The Porno Pal System–advertising mostly in the back pages of skin magazines as well as The Christian Science Monitor–he had taken on just about every client imaginable. Rabbis with foot fetishes. Rich WASPy CEOs stockpiling pictures of pregnant, lactating black women. High school gym teachers with extensive collections of S&M tableaux. You name it. And Guy had never once felt the compulsion to check up on anybody. But this guy Cooley had him spooked. This doughy white face was infesting Guy's dreams. What in God's name could this jerk be hiding in the bowels of his home?

For an entire week, moving through his daily routine with zombie-like complacency, Guy got up every morning, had breakfast with Karen, and went to work (for years, Karen Fox had been operating under the false impression that her husband had been running a small research firm, and Guy had seen no reason to correct her). It was a relatively uneventful week, too, with only a few new clients and one death/retrieval scenario (a straight-forward job removing hardcore gay porn from the nooks and crannies of a Catholic rectory). Every night, Guy would come home exhausted. Not from the work but rather from the rumination. The image of Cooley's red-rimmed eyes and yellow smile was just too creepy for Guy to shake.

On the last evening before Guy finally did something about

his suspicions, his parents were visiting. The Douche King rarely graced Guy and Karen with personal visits, but this week had been different. Guy's parents had been over a few days earlier to show slides from their trip to Branson, Missouri, and now, tonight, they had returned with paint swaths from Sherman Williams in order to help Karen choose a color for the spare room. For some reason, Guy's mother was harboring the delusion that this room might become a nursery. Little did the older woman know the longing, the misery, the ongoing angst between Guy and Karen about having children. Notwithstanding his mysterious impotence, Guy dreaded the prospect of having kids. He adored children–as did Karen – but he was also terrified of bringing one into this world, what with all the shit, the lies and secrets, metastasizing in the dark like some kind of cancer.

"Now explain to me again the meaning of this piece," the Douche King was saying in his patented smug style, standing in Guy's living room, staring at the missing children collage on the wall, while Karen chattered away out in the kitchen with Guy's mother. The Douche King was a tall, lanky man with a head full of lustrous silver waves. He had a long Patrician nose down which he would view most of the world, considering the bulk of it beneath him. He never really "got" Karen's art.

"I guess it's a statement on all the injustices meted out to kids in this world," Guy surmised, standing behind his dad with his hands in his pockets. The "piece" that they were referring to was titled Lost Visage Number 13, and was basically a 4-by-4 foot piece of foam core plastered with a matrix of missing children. Blurry faces of kids from milk cartons all chockablock across a grey field.

The Douche King pointed his aquiline beak at Guy. "I don't get it."

Guy shrugged. "I guess it's not for everybody."

"Thank God for that," the older man mused, giving the artwork one last glance.

That night, Guy jerked awake from a vague and troubling nightmare. In the dream he had been scratching a hole in himself with a rolled up porn magazine, the wound opening like a vulva, dripping a white, viscous fluid. Heart thumping, flabby body filmed with sweat, Guy shook off the disorienting dread and climbed out of bed.

He got dressed quietly, careful not to awaken Karen, then slipped out the side door. The interior of his car was as cold as a meat locker.

It was dawn by the time he arrived at Fifth Third Bank, the pale light glowing on the edges of the horizon, the air redolent with that sweet, dewy smell familiar only to fishermen, civil servants and methedrine addicts. He waited for forty-five minutes for the morning watchman to arrive and open the doors.

It took some talking to convince the safe deposit manager that there had been a mistake with Cooley's document package and Guy was merely "straightening out the paperwork." The manager finally let Guy into the box room, where Guy stood in the blazing fluorescent light, slipping the map of Cooley's house and the front door key into his briefcase.

Over the entire history of Guy's modest little enterprize, he had never attempted to get into a client's house prior to their death. This was wrong on so many levels. But Guy didn't care. He had never been so completely repulsed by the mere presence of a client.

Cooley's house was in an elite white collar enclave on the north shore called Indian Hills: Miles of labyrinthine lanes bordered by stately mansions, manicured lawns, and cobblestone driveways that virtually screamed "Big Money."

Guy waited a half a block away from Cooley's gorgeous three-story until the entire Cooley clan gradually drifted out the front door for their day's activities. Cooley came first – his cadaverous face in shadow, his lanky body clad in a suit and tie – hauling a briefcase off to some innocuous middle-management job. Then came mom and the kids. Squeaky-clean and freshly-scrubbed all. Like an ad for Martha Stewart's Living.

When the house was empty, Guy calmly strode up the walk and gained entrance.

At first Guy was stricken by the positively average quality of the place. He wasn't sure what he had expected...but certainly not this. The rooms were neat and well furnished, but nothing ostentatious. Tidy Scandinavian design furniture and signs of happy children all over the place. Toy boxes, and finger paintings on the refrigerator. Aquariums bubbling cheerfully. The air smelled of soap and cookies and floor wax. This was not the home of a monster.

Guy went downstairs. The basement was a cozy, finished play room, toys neatly stowed in cabinets, tasteful, burnt umber wall-to-wall. Guy looked at the map again – a Xerox reduction of an architectural floor plan – which notated the stash in the basement. But something was wrong. The pornography was supposed to be in a shelving unit right here.

Pausing, Guy looked at the northeast corner of the room. There was a big screen TV and a book case filled with kid videos such as Shrek and The Lion King. But no stash. Not even the possibility of a stash.

A muffled click.

Guy jerked around, looking for the source of the sound, the faint clicking noise. He was jumpy now. He heard the noise again, and this time it seemed to be coming from underneath the floor. Guy blinked. He looked at the map again. Then he looked down at the floor. The realization struck him like an ice pick to the back of his neck. The stash was in a sub level. A crawlspace perhaps. A sub-basement.

He started nosing around the heating ducts, along the baseboard and behind the furniture. He consulted the map and extrapolated from Cooley's notations. Finally he found a loose panel in the southwest corner. He was about to push it inward when he heard the clicking noise again, closer, more pronounced, almost like a match-tip being struck.

Whirling toward the noise, Guy saw nothing. The room was empty. But something was wrong. There was something different about the room. Guy looked down at the carpet. In the middle of the room, on the floor, there lay a single Polaroid photograph. Had Guy missed it before? Not likely. Gooseflesh rashing up his back, he went over to the Polaroid, picked it up, and looked at it.

His throat went dry.

It was still developing, still milky and faded, but slowly coming into focus: A photograph of Guy, crouching down in the corner of the basement, fiddling with the loose panel, preparing to push it in.

It was a photograph taken only moments ago.

"Very good then!"

The voice blurted from somewhere behind him, and Guy spun around reflexively –

– and what he saw standing there at the base of the stairs fifteen feet away was for some reason almost beyond his powers of comprehension: A pale, wrinkled figure in a pink marbled spandex suit holding an old fashioned Polaroid Land camera.

Click-whirrrrrrr! A flash in Guy's eyes, momentarily blinding him.

Then things were happening all at once, very quickly, in the silver blur of Guy's compromised vision: another photo oozing from the camera, and Guy jerking backward as he realized that this man wasn't wearing spandex at all, in fact, this man wasn't wearing anything. Cooley's pale nude body was spattered with blood, and he was holding a Taser gun in his other hand – the same kind of small electric cattle prod that police use nowadays to control unruly mobs.

"No wait no – !" Guy slammed backward into the flimsy wall at the precise moment a tendril of blue voltage arced out of the muzzle of the Taser.

The wall cracked under Guy's weight as electricity pierced him, making his fingers curl into claws. The wall opened with a sudden groan, the cheap panel snapping, and Guy tumbled backward into the dark, flailing his rigid arms. All he could see was a silver vein of light across his eyes as he plunged into the rotting shadows.

He landed with a thud on cold stone, literally gasping with shock.

There are so many flavors of pain, from the sharp, sudden sensation of a splinter under a nail to the dull, throbbing agonies of major surgery. But landing hard on the spur of one's tailbone on a surface such as stone elicits the full panorama these sensations all at once.

Guy lay there in the darkness writhing in a tidal wave of pain. In fact, it took him several seconds – very long seconds – to even draw a breath. Capillaries of light seethed across his eyeballs, the high voltage shock still strangling him as he finally gulped a lungful of air. He curled into a fetal position and let out a spontaneous mewl, holding his lower back. The pain was a tympany drum in his head now. He swallowed and tried to sit up but could only manage to get up on one elbow. The feeling was gradually coming back into his hands and feet.

In the shifting, yellow light of a swinging bare bulb, Guy tried to focus on something. Anything. And it took several moments for his eyes to register the images.

Cooley's gallery was taped and pasted and thumb-tacked across every available inch of the moldy, unfinished walls. Many more of the photographs were neatly boxed and stacked on rusted metal shelves. Here was the stash which Guy had been contracted to retrieve. But these were more than mere pornographic pictures. These were trophies of some sort. Documentation of Cooley's lifelong perversions.

Guy heard heavy footsteps padding down a ladder behind him, and he tried to move but couldn't make his legs work properly. The pain was shackling his pelvis and his heart was racing so swiftly he could barely think but there was something about the profusion of pictures that was driving Guy on.

He noticed a row of photos taped to the ceiling beam above him and his heart contracted into a stone. He recognized some of the faces. Innocent, wide-eyed faces. Some of them school photos. Some of them cropped from family photos. The milk carton children.

The missing.

All of them victims of a doughy-faced insurance executive named Herbert Cooley –

– who was, at this very moment, reaching the bottom of a step ladder on the far side of the crawlspace. Guy could hear his watery, heavy breathing. The tazer was making a faint crackling noise.

Guy tried to rise but it was futile. The torment of his spine and the partial paralysis kept him glued to his ass on the moist floor of the crawlspace, surrounded by the litter of a compulsive masturbator. Empty bottles of lubricant. Soiled blankets and towels. A space heater rattling, the cozy orange glow for those wintery evenings of self-abuse.

Some of the pictures – the worst ones – showed the young victims bound and gagged. Guy wondered if there were tiny bones buried somewhere?

A photo screamed at Guy from the wall to his right, a wallet sized black-and-white photo of a two-year-old boy, pasted on yellow ruled paper, an edging of compulsive doodles around it – flowers and penises and skulls – all of it flooding Guy with memories.

As a toddler Guy had slightly crossed eyes for which he wore corrective glasses from pre-school through the second grade. Right now, at this very moment, this same cross-eyed child was staring out from a black and white snapshot taken on some discount store carousel.

The picture was worse than a Taser shock, jolting Guy with a primal memory:

Alone in an empty Corvair, in the darkness, terrified, sobbing, snot on his face, shackled to his car seat, mommy's door open, steam coming out of the car, and mommy out on the road, in the rain, waving at lights. The little boy cannot see her anymore. A scream, and then nothing but mist on the windows. The little boy sobs. And then, and then, and then – the moment that will change the little boy's life forever – the side door opens and a ghostly man appears, a very pale, tall man with red-rimmed eyes. "Very good then," he says, and reaches in and takes the boy. The boy is flailing and screaming. The pale man gets rough. Throws the boy in a dark trunk. And hours go by. Finally the trunk opens in a silent, dark place that smells of oil and chalk, and the man tries to lift the boy out. But the boy gets lucky. The boy bites into the man's wrist, and the man screams, and the boy manages to slip away and run across a dark place. The boy sees an opening and squeezes through it, then tears out into the night. Into the rain. Toward the closest house. Toward safety –

– and back in the here and now, lying supine in a puddle of God-knows-what – urine? – semen? – an overturned vanilla Slim-Fast shake? – Guy put the sudden revelation out of his mind. The fleeting realization that this was how Guy became an orphan, and this why Cooley had set off internal alarms when Guy had first met him – all of it – was short lived...because Guy had more pressing matters facing him at the current moment: trapped in a hellish subterranean museum, a naked pedophile approaching with a crackling Taser gun.

"I wondered how long it would take for you to get curious,"

Cooley mused as he towered over Guy, a pair of objects now aimed directly at Guy – the buzzing muzzle of a Taser gun and a crooked, veined, purple erection.

"Okay, look, let me go and, and, and – " Guy started to stammer but suddenly saw an opportunity that would probably only be available for a very brief instant.

Cooley was licking his lips. "It certainly took me long enough to find you."

"Don't do this," Guy pleaded, but it was all acting now because Guy saw his only chance plugged into an exposed duplex outlet mounted on the moldy wall-board ten feet away.

"You were the only one," Cooley wanted Guy to know.

"The only one what?"

"The only one that got away," Cooley said with that cadaverous grin. In the gloom of the crawlspace, his teeth were the color of spoiled egg yolks.

"How did you – ?

Cooley aimed the Taser at Guy's face. "The irony! After all these years, I finally find you, and look at the service you're providing!"

"Wait, wait – "

"Pity you won't to be able to fulfill the covenants of our agreement."

Just as Cooley was about to pull the trigger, Guy kicked the space heater over.

The glowing grille of the heater landed on the milky fluid on the floor.

Cooley's hand froze suddenly on the Taser, the muzzle spitting a tendril of lightning off into the shadows as the space heater boiled with sparks at his feet. Guy had to shield his face as a sheath of electricity flickered up Cooley's nude, varicose form, sending him into shuddering spasms. His mouth gaped. His blood-shot eyes bulged, and a blue flame licked up the back of his head, catching the delicate wisps of grey hair there. The stench of cooking meat was overwhelming.

Guy managed to roll away as the naked pedophile was fried to a crisp.

The conductor: Cooley's own watery spoor, his own ritual ejaculate.

Guy covered his face until the crackling stopped and silence returned to that terrible place.

*　*　*　*　*

The unmarked squad car smelled of stale cigar smoke and wintergreen deodorizer. Guy sat in the back behind the metal screen, wrapped in a woolen blanket. Through the window he could see the EMS attendants carrying Cooley's body – now covered with a sheet – across the lawn. In the pre-dawn gloom, the neighbors were gathered behind yellow tape, shaking their heads and clucking their tongues at such a spectacle unfolding in their gorgeous hermetically-sealed world.

"About this so-called service you were talking about in your statement," the cop in the front seat was saying. He was plainclothes. Fifty-ish, bad sport coat, calloused gaze. He shot a look over the seat back at Guy.

"The Porno Pal System," Guy murmured, his forehead resting on the grimy rear window.

"Yeah, right. The Porno Pal System." The cop smiled wanly, scratching his bad buzz cut, obviously measuring his words. "Let's talk about that for a second."

"I'm closing our doors," Guy mumbled.

"What was that?"

Guy looked at the detective, wondering what kind of charges would be leveled against this clandestine little company. "I'm officially going out of business."

"Is that right?"

Guy nodded.

The cop shrugged, then gazed back out the front window. "That's a shame," he said, starting the engine. "I was going to sign up for it myself."

Guy didn't say anything.

"Give you a ride home?" the cop asked.

Guy said that would be great, then stared back out the window as the car pulled away from the death house...

...and made its way back through the labyrinth of graceful old homes, their tasteful draperies and blinds drawn across their tasteful bay windows, ever obscuring the outer world from the secrets within.

DEAL MEMO

APPLEBAUM STEINBERG & FRISHMAN LLP.
2100 Alameda Boulevard – Beverly Hills, CA 90211

As of October 1, 2004

Mr. Howard Miller, Executive Producer
Icon Productions
34 West Canal
Brisbane, AUSTRALIA 445BT
RE: THE PASSION OF THE CHRIST

Dear Mr. Miller:

The underlying agreement shall heretofore formalize all previous discussions with principal parties in connection with the sequel and/or sequels based on the original motion picture titled THE PASSION OF THE CHRIST ("THE PROPERTY").

This includes, but is not limited to, all spin-off characters and situations based on the screenplay and/or original source material (AKA "THE BIBLE"), as well as all future ancillary rights and tie-ins based on the aforementioned material, including, but not limited to, computer software, CDs, DVDs, toys, internet programming, action figures, live performances, musical productions, breakfast cereals, ice-capades, kids meals, triple-X adult movies, and any other merchandise, product, or artifact that could conceivably be conceived to tie-in with the "Work," in this universe, as well as the kingdom of heaven and earth, for all time.

This agreement shall be between Mr. Mel Gibson ("ARTIST") and the entity known as Satan ("THE COMPANY") (also known as Beelzebub, Lucifer, Prince of Darkness, or the Walt Disney Corporation). The terms listed below shall supercede all other contractual agreements to date, and hold harmless "THE COMPANY" from any responsibility whatsoever in the event of anything whatsoever, including acts of God and/or apocalyptic intervention.

Upon signing of this agreement in human blood, verified by notary public, the above parties agree to the following:

1) The "ARTIST" shall deliver a completed print of the first sequel (the "PROPERTY") on or before the deadline date 18 months from the execution of this agreement (in human blood) in consideration of the sum of one trillion dollars (American), undiminished sexual prowess, and eternal life.

2) The "PROPERTY" shall be released under the following title in 78-point blood-spatter type font:
PASSION TWO: UNDEAD & MAD AS HELL

3) Further, the "ARTIST" agrees that the content of the "PROPERTY" shall adhere to the story line approved in writing by the "COMPANY" upon commencement of principal photography (*see Addendum/Table 1 for a synopsis).

4) In order to achieve maximum turn-over and concession sales the "PROPERTY" shall be no longer than 78 minutes in duration, and shall contain a minimum of one (1) product placement per minute of screen time (*see Addendum/Table 2 for a list of sanctioned products).

5) The final soundtrack of the "PROPERTY" shall contain a minimum of one complete pop song per scene, each approved for airplay and/or tie-in CD – the net proceeds of which will be split evenly (50/50) between the "ARTIST" and SATAN (or Satan's agents on earth; i.e., The Walt Disney Company) (**See Addendum/Table 3 for a list of sanctioned songs).

6) The "ARTIST" agrees to embed a minimum of one (1) subliminal message every two minutes within the frames of the completed final print of the "PROPERTY" (***See Addendum/Table 4 for list of approved messages).

7) The final release print of the "PROPERTY" shall be screened only in approved multiplexes owned by the "COMPANY" with a minimum of seventy-two (72) screens, and shall run continuously, 24 hours per day, 7 days per week, with start times staggered every 15 minutes.

8) The advertising/promotion budget for said release of the "PROPERTY" shall be no less than eighty-six trillion dollars ($86,000,000,000,000) and no more than...well, infinity.

9) Further, upon the release of the home video version, the "street date" of the release shall be delayed for a minimum of 12 months (to a maximum of 3 years), during which time a blanket media campaign will profile the forthcoming release as a special "one-time-only" opportunity to "own Jesus" before "He" returns to "the Disney vaults" forever and ever. (Note: All prints and advertising will feature the tag line "He's baaaaack, and this time it's personal!")

This Agreement, upon execution, shall be in full force and effect, and supercede all other agreements and contracts between the two parties (except that previous deal regarding an Oscar for BRAVEHEART...which is okay with "COMPANY" if Gibson wants to keep that one in place). The parties hereto indicate their agreement and acceptance of the forgoing by signing in human blood at the places provided below.

ACCEPTED AND AGREED:

ICON FILM PRODUCTIONS LMTD.
By: _____
Its: _____

_____
Mel Gibson

THE WALT DISNEY COMPANY LMTD.
By: _____
Its:_____

_____
"The Devil" – President/CEO – Kingdom of Darkness

ADDENDUM – TABLE 1
APPROVED STORY SYNOPSIS
"PASSION II: UNDEAD AND MAD AS HELL"

After being tortured by psychotic Centurians, crucified and left for dead, the troubled yet sexy young carpenter, Jesus Christ, is sealed inside a moldering cave with nothing left but his wits, a peek-a-boo loin cloth, and some heavy duty mojo. Everybody thinks this is the end of Jesus…but this is only the beginning! Christ is risen, baby, and he's pissed off! The Prince of Peace becomes a hip, deadly zombie assassin with a taste for fast chariots, fast harlots, and faster revenge. And he's got the Big Man behind him! Hey Rome – put this in your temple and smoke it! Jesus is baaaaaack!!!

ADDENDUM – TABLE 2
SANCTIONED PRODUCT PLACEMENTS

1. Las Vegas Visitors and Tourist Bureau
2. Cheech Marin's Big Bootie Bongs and Hash Pipes™
3. Lee Press-On Nails™
4. Sammy Hagar's Cabo Wabo Resort and Spa™
5. Kalishnakov Fine Hand-Tooled Assault Rifles™
6. Philip Morris All-Natural Organic Cigarettes™
7. Grand Theft Auto V for PlayStation™
8. Girls Gone Wild Productions™
9. National Association of Cosmetic Surgeons
10. Carl Sagan's Easy Evolution for Children from Crown Books™
11. Fredericks of Hollywood™
12. Branson, Missouri, Chamber of Commerce
13. Chicken Ranch Brothels and Spas™
14. Binions Casinos
15. 'E' Entertainment Television™
16. World Wrestling Federation
17. Hapscolme's Tactor Pulls and Demolition Derbies™
18. Hostess Twinkies
19. "Barely Legal" Volumes 1-23 Collectors' DVDs™
20. Veal Producers' Association
21. American Telemarketers' Association
22. Spice™ Pay-For-View Systems, Inc.
23. Magic Fingers™ Beds and Mattresses
24. Fox Television, Inc.
25. Tony Robbins Motivational Workshops™

ADDENDUM – TABLE 3
APPROVED SONGS FOR SOUNDTRACK

1. "Sympathy for the Devil" by the Rolling Stones (Mr. Richards certainly owes "COMPANY" a favor)
2. Anything by Black Sabbath
3. "Pour Some Sugar on Me" by Def Leppard
4. "Smell the Glove" by Spinal Tap
5. "I'm Too Sexy" by Right Said Fred
6. Anything by Prince (up until he converted to Christianity)
7. "Cop Killah" by NWA
8. "Sex and Drugs and Rock and Roll" by Ian Dury and the Blockheads
9. "Big 10-Inch Record" by Aerosmith
10. "Sex Machine" by James Brown
11. "I Touch Myself" by The Divinyls
12. "Like a Virgin" by Madonna (also on contract)
13. "Titties and Beer" by Frank Zappa
14. "Let's Get it On" by Marvin Gaye
15. "Son of a Preacher Man" by Bobbie Gentry
16. "Belly of the Beast" by Anthrax
17. "I Wanna Rock" by Twisted Sister
18. "Cherry Pie" by Warrant
19. Anything by Iron Maiden
20. "Dr. Feelgood" by Motley Crew
21. "Talk Dirty to Me" by Poison
22. "Highway to Hell" by AC/DC
23. "Super Freak" by Rick James (also owes Lucifer a favor)
24. "Welcome to the Jungle" by Guns 'n' Roses
25. "Symphony of Destruction" by Megadeth

Gibson Deal Memo (cont.)

ADDENDUM – TABLE 4
APPROVED SUBLIMINAL MESSAGES

1. "Hail Satan"
2. "Relax, consume, shop – everything's going to be fine"
3. "Drive SUVs"
4. "Eat more carbs"
5. "The Moral Majority is neither moral nor a majority – discuss amongst yourselves"
6. "Billy Graham wears a thong"
7. "Church is for Pussies"
8. "Jerry Springer for President"
9. "War is good"
10. "O.J. was innocent"
11. "Screw the poor"
12. "Buy Enron stocks"
13. "Sin Rocks!"
14. "Ozzy Osbourne is God"
15. "Violence is sexy!"
16. "A Mind is a Great Thing to Waste"
17. "Greed is Good"
18. "What Global Warming?"
19. "Drugs are for Kids"
20. "Shoot Now, Think Later"
21. "Play on the Highway"
22. "Drive Faster"
23. "Stop Calling Your Mother"
24. "Reading is NOT fundamental"
25. "Drop the Big One Now!"

L-R: Jay Bonansinga, John Everson, Martin Mundt, Bill Breedlove